CAUGHT INSIDE

A SURFING PASSAGE

LAUREN BENTON ANGULO

ISBN-10: 0615629172
EAN-13: 9780615629179
Library of Congress Control Number: 2012906702
SurferSeen Inc., Hanalei HAWAII

"The Hawaiian method proposes that wave size be measured from the back. It usually results in an estimation less than half that of a face measurement. Coming into use during the 1960s, the Hawaiian method apparently was adopted as psychological intimidation of inexperienced visitors."

Willard Bascom
Estimating Breaking Wave Height
www.surfresearch.com.au

Wave heights, for the purpose of this story, are reported using the Hawaiian method. A wave described as "four foot" has a wave face between eight and ten feet.

.

CHAPTER 1

KAIMANA JOSHUA KELLER
THURSDAY, JANUARY 14, 1:00 P.M.

It seemed like the perfect surf session.

An overhead swell arrived earlier than predicted on Surfline, the clouds had cleared, and light offshore winds were blowing, along with peeling barrels that spit every other wave.

At the start of fourth period, all Hanalei and Haena students were summoned to the North Shore school busses. Foretelling the bridge closure, the river gauge was steadily rising due to the converging high tide, incoming swell, and non-stop rain. I was gratefully home hours earlier than usual.

I hadn't been able to surf on a school day since I stayed home sick two years ago and talked my mom into letting me get wet, even though I'd thrown up three times.

Today, the water is pale-ale brown due to the rain-swollen rivers from continuous downpours of the past few days. Pieces of branches and debris pop up in and around the lineup. It's visually uninviting, but still a sight for sore eyes, and arriving home early to surf is karmic payback for surviving a tough first half of the week: I blew a geometry test, lost my lunch card, and was called a mini-menehune by a senior in front of a hot sophomore girl. I might be one of the shorter freshmen, but I've got some guns and a six-pack and I'm one of the best surfers in the school. Still, girls listen to what senior boys say, so that sucked.

I wax my board, deck pad, and the top of my feet. I attach the Velcro leash strap around my right ankle while hopping down the beach, sprint the last fifty feet to the ocean, launch myself over the shore pound to the sheet-glass section behind the brown froth, and start the relatively short paddle out.

Pine Trees is my home break and I live less than a half-mile away. My dad initiated me to big-wave duck-diving at this beach break on a four-foot NW swell. He wore swim fins and pushed my four-foot six-inch surfboard and me into waves I thought were gigantic. I remember I scrambled up to my feet, spread my legs wide, and gripped so hard with my toes that my feet ached for days. After he pushed me into the wave, he swam in and helped me paddle back out, using his weight and strength to fluidly duck-dive us through double overhead waves that no other kid my age would even consider. I was seven years old then. I won my first contest at Pine Trees when I was nine. I belong in this lineup, on this wave, in this particular part of the ocean. It's not that I have a sense of ownership of this break — this wave owns *me*, it calls my name, and I always respond like a well-trained pet.

There are only three guys out. No groms in the water. With older surfers in the lineup, I'm guessing they'll sit on the outside waiting for the bigger sets and regretfully allow a lot of good waves to go by.

I was surfing with my mom once and I asked her why she was so selective about the peaks she tried to catch. She replied, "I have to pick my waves — just like I pick my battles with you." I guess it's an adult-lack-of-energy thing, which is one aspect of growing up that I can't imagine ever happening to me. I can tirelessly surf for three to five hours at a time, and my record is ten hours in one day. I probably caught a hundred waves that day, and I would have kept surfing, but it was pitch-black out, and I was so hungry I considered eating half an old musubi I found on the beach as I was walking home.

Making my way to the lineup, a few waves roll past me and I imagine myself riding each one: drop-in, snap, snap, carve, pull in, spit out. A Christmas-morning-when-I-was-five anticipation rolls through me and I smile, creasing my sun-blocked face.

Paddling toward the regular peak, with currents of colder-than-usual water shocking my skin, I hear the familiar whistle signaling a bigger set approaching. I know the next swell is showing six feet, NW swell, fourteen-second intervals on the buoys. The whistle must mean the approaching swell is sending out early pulses. Still, I don't expect to see a dark lump at Manalau, the outer reef, rising up and feathering.

I drop my head, dig my arms deeply into the water, and paddle "like I mean it" to get farther out in time to either catch a wave, or at least spare myself from getting pounded on the inside.

Hustling to get up and over the first set wave, I catch a glimpse of one of the guys who spent some time on the tour making a late drop and immediately pulling in. I slow my paddling and watch as he gets fully domed, racing toward the light through the dark cavern. My second's hesitation to watch him means I have to duck-dive a big lip as the same wave throws a foot in front of me.

The two other surfers half-heartedly jockey for position on the next outside wave, and as I paddle over the third shoulder, I see with my bird's-eye view the biggest wave in the set hurtling inward from the outside.

If I'm going to catch the wave, I have only a few seconds to paddle out toward the forming peak. As the last outside potential rider turns toward the horizon, broadcasting his decision to let this wave pass, I fully commit and make a beeline straight for where I envision the peak will rise up and start its final hurl toward the beach. My timing is right-on; I spin around as the wave hits the sandbar and thrusts an eight-foot peaky face directly behind my left shoulder. Digging deeper, fully bound in partnership with this singular wave, I catch the surge and feel the momentary thrilling loss of gravity as the wave pulls me in and starts to throw. I'm on my feet, crouched low; the wave hollows out from the drop and envelops me in a circular greenish-brown room. A sweet sensation of complete calm floods through me as I realize I'm locked and loaded on a flawless barrel. The ocean's voice switches from a roar to rushing silence, the texture and color of the water is vibrantly magnified, a whiff of sea turtle mixes in with the salt air, time slows to a uniquely tubular dimension, and all is right in the world.

Immediately after I experience nirvana (which should have been followed by my re-entering the real world by being spit out, punching through the back of the tube, or worst case, straightening out and taking a pounding inside) my reality skips a section, like an edit-delete in iMovie. I open my eyes while I cartwheel underwater, assess the pressure in my ears, and place myself more than ten feet down, and experience a dreadful awareness of zero oxygen in my lungs.

The voice in my head wildly accuses, "How did this happen, what's going on?"

Every muscle strains to reach for the surface, but my mind commands my body to relax. There's no use fighting a wave that's holding me down. The ocean wins every time. Even in previous two-wave hold-downs, I haven't felt this lightheaded or panicked about not having air. Instinctively, I pull my knees up near my belly and keep my arms loosely folded around my tucked and throbbing head, blocking at least part of my body from impact with my board and the sandy, almost-concrete ocean floor.

I sense the slight change in water pressure above me, and I start to kick and scratch my way to the light of the sky. As I uncurl my legs, plant my feet, and push off the bottom, a wide stream of bright-red blood whooshes past my face. My sight line to the surface blurs, replaced by dimly flashing starbursts of light. My muscles stop exerting effort, my arms and legs go limp, and my determination to stay conscious vanishes.

CHAPTER 2

KEKOA MALEKO JONES
THURSDAY, JANUARY 14, 12:45 P.M.

Finally, an afternoon off from that crappy job.

Pulling into the Pine Trees parking lot, I notice only three other guys out in the water, and they're basically kooks. No groms yet, thank God. Those kids are such a pain in the ass. They're like mosquitoes, buzzing around in the water, making noise, and getting in the way. Instead of real surfing, they remind me of circus dogs doing tricks. They're mostly spoiled brats — with new equipment, coaches, and parents that drive them around the island every day looking for the best waves.

The buzz in the coffee shop this morning was that a substantial swell showed up on the radar. It used to be you had to go look at the ocean to see if there was surf. Nowadays, any idiot with an Internet connection can find out when there are waves arriving, from which direction, and how big, steep, and clean they'll be. I heard the coffee server say the swell is supposed to arrive early tomorrow. What would she know? Another chick surfer: Why can't they just stay on the beach, looking good in bikinis? They gotta surf, too?

Well, lucky me; the swell *is* early. Actually, I'm not lucky at all, but maybe this is karmic payoff for making it through a brutal half-week; I screwed up a cut on a plank of koa that cost me $400, left my ATM card at Big Save, and was called a dumbass by my boss in front of the good-looking homeowner whose house we're remodeling. I might have made a "measure twice, cut once" mistake, but I'm fairly smart and I know I'm a great surfer. Not that either matters anymore, since the attractive, animal-doctor homeowner has no interest in talking to me, and I'm no longer involved in the surf industry. My life pretty much sucks — with the exception of surfing — and even that is becoming as disappointing as my last two girlfriends.

The water looks more like this morning's coffee than my khaki-green carpenter pants. There's some crap bobbing around in the lineup, possibly literally, but it's probably just sticks and river runoff. I used to love surfing this wave. I remember getting pumped up on the walk down He'e Road from Weke and spying the rolling, undulating ocean past the raised-dirt parking lot.

Pine Trees is my home break. I taught myself how to surf here — first on a bodyboard, and then using a beat-up, six-foot swallowtail I found in the trash at a friend's house. The board was missing one of its three glassed-on fins, and it wasn't the center fin. Pine Trees is primarily a right break, which was fortunate because that was the only direction I could go without sliding out on a bottom

12

turn. I've always felt comfortable surfing this break. Even when I traveled the world on the tour, I anticipated every return trip to Kauai and would carve out time for a Pine Trees session. No one treated me differently when I came home. It was the same as when I was a kid, like any other surfer who loves Kauai and loves surfing. Even as one of the first kids from the Garden Isle — other than Andy and Bruce — to make it to the WCT, the local crew welcomed me back but still made me earn my waves, just like everyone else.

Things are different now — both for me and for pro surfing. The tour is about tricks and politics and bullshit, which doesn't play to my strong suits. Not that I had a choice. I didn't make the cut eight years ago, and my lifelong dream of being a pro surfer evaporated. It's not unusual for a rookie to not make it past his first year, but other guys didn't have to deal with the rules and judging criteria changing. It was unfair to surfers like me who had spent their lives honing big turns and barrel riding. I was late to the tour anyway because I spent time doing the Junior Pro and then the QS circuit. It seemed as if all the other wannabe pro surfers kept up to speed on the evolving changes, especially the Brazilians and Australians, but that Hawaiians stayed focused on the beauty and strength of our art, which caused some of us to miss the signs that professional surfing was progressing in a different direction. We all grew up surfing waves of consequence — big, intense, open-ocean swell — that aren't the standard fare on the tour. Born and raised surfing in Hawaii makes a person a stronger waterman, a bigger charger, a deeper barrel rider, and, in my opinion, an all-around better surfer. Even as a kid, competing in Southern California at the NSSA Nationals, I remember the not-so-subtly-hidden fear and frustration aimed at me and the other kids from the fiftieth state. I recall hearing the disappointed hissing, "The Hawaiians are here," from Southern and Northern Cali groms as we paddled out to Lowers or Salt Creek for our warm-up sessions.

I can whine and bitch for hours about the disappointments and unfair stuff that has happened to me, but I'm here now and there's a new swell showing early, so I'm taking advantage of the fact that the masses of locals and tourists haven't arrived yet to ruin it for me.

When there's a rising swell like this, I like to check out the waves without duck-diving a lot to get to the lineup, so I walk down the beach and paddle out in the channel between Pine Trees and The Cape. This view allows me to see the shape of the wave from the back. If it's barreling, as it appears to have the potential to do today, I get superstitious and don't like to see the inside of the tube until I'm in it.

Making my way to the takeoff spot, I hear one of the kooks in the lineup whistling wildly. It's not big yet, and he doesn't have to have a tizzy because a set's coming. But as I glide over an inside wave, I notice spray coming off the top of a feathering peak out back. How can Manalau be breaking? My mind justifies that it might be a sneaker wave from the coming swell. Since Manalau's feathering, it will be a solid four to five footer by the time it rolls into Pine Trees. My body shifts into contest-heat gear. There's a different paddling speed I acquired while competing, and now I'm breathing short, hard bursts like I'm sprinting up a flight of stairs. I used to train every day, running, swimming, jiu-jitsu, and of course, surfing. Now my day consists of work, Fuel TV, and video games. I surf only when I see myself in my usual slack-faced, crumpled posture and am willing to force myself off the couch and drive to a break.

Muscle memory is a powerful thing, and having surfed for almost thirty years, my brain automatically calculates the speed, size, and shape of the approaching wave. Predictably, the kooks missed it. They're too busy whistling and nervously paddling out, so it's wide open and calling my name like a mother I never knew.

To get to the wave, I quickly stroke farther out and to my left, directly toward the spot where I know it will hit the sandbar and pitch. I prefer to come at this wave from the back, behind the peak, but the swell direction and the way the bar is shaped looks a little different from the usual Pine Trees. There's no room for error, as there is only a small, workable entrance point. This particular wave's developing shape is setting up a steep, hollow, lightening-fast opening section. My mind shifts from mental thoughts to my body-brain as my right arm pulls deeper in the water angling my board almost parallel with the forming peak; as the rolling mound of seawater hits the sandbar and jacks straight up, I paddle in.

There's a second of free falling as I airdrop into the pocket and set my inside fin and rail. All thinking stops as the wave grabs, holds, and launches me in what feels like slow motion but is actually a lightning-fast tube ride. What heroin is to drugs, barrels are to surfing. If Surfer's Anonymous existed, I would be obligated to stand up and say, "My name is Kekoa, and I'm a tubeaholic."

A barrel is my own private sensory-deprivation room in which I feel a maximum awareness in every cell: It provides a deafeningly loud silence in which I possess cave-dark laser sight and feel a sense of total relaxation while I'm completely amped out. I've been in thousands of tubes, and every one is simultaneously thrilling and completely calming. As Billabong's slogan arrogantly claims, "Only a surfer knows the feeling." Yeah, they got that right.

As I shift a little weight to my front foot, the board accelerates and, with the help of a burst of spit, I fly out of the barrel into the daylight.

Catching the first wave in a set is both a blessing and a curse. There's no backwash or turbulence from a previous wave. On the other hand, there are the remaining waves to contend with, and this appears to be a solid lumbering set, judging from the lines rolling in at Manalau and the next wave heaving and throwing on the sandbar. I could wait on the inside until the set passes, but real surfers don't do that — they paddle back out, through whatever the ocean serves up.

As I near the fourth and largest wave in the set, I catch a glimpse of a surfer in the barrel. Where did that guy come from? He didn't catch it from the outside. He must have been paddling out, at the same time as me, but from the usual Pine Trees parking lot channel. It's a sweet barrel, symmetrically round, and he's comfortably holding a stylish stance, dragging his arm to get as much time behind the curtain as possible; his face emanates pure bliss. My mind records that video clip as I start my duck-dive. Catching a last peek of his barrel ride as I push the nose of my board deep into the shoulder of the same wave, my brain registers something strange. I can't quite process what is weird, but something is wrong with the last nanosecond of my peripheral view of the surfer. I recall a fatal car accident I observed a few years ago when a motorcycle sped through a yellow-lit intersection and was clipped by an SUV that appeared out of nowhere. I had that same feeling of, "What the … ?"

I don't usually pay attention to anyone else in the water, but as I punch through the back of the wave, I pause to glance over my shoulder and confirm that the surfer kicked out. I know I have only seconds until the next big wave rolls in. Twisting my head further, I don't see him shoot over the back of the froth. So, he didn't make the barrel. No big deal. Most people don't. He seemed to have the correct line with his rail planing at the right height and angle, and I expected him to come flying out over the back of the wave. Maybe it pinched at the end: It happens. I start to paddle again, but something forces me to look back just to see the surfer pop up inside after getting pounded by the wave. Strange, though, there's no one there. It's almost like I imagined him. I never saw him in the lineup. I never saw him paddle out. I never saw him catch the wave. I thought I saw a surfer in the barrel and now there's no one.

Just to convince myself I'm not crazy, I hesitate a few more seconds and scan the ocean from the white wash to the beach. No one is there. I've duck-dived three waves, and I don't know anyone who can make it through a three-wave hold down. What was that weird vision, or feeling, I had just before the surfer was out of my sight? My mind replays the last split-second frame. I can see it clearly now: He fell forward as if he had been sucker punched from behind. I know the wave didn't clip him. There was ample room in that barrel; he could have waved his arms over his head and not touched the water.

Shit.

That's all I can think as I turn my board toward the shore and go in search of the surfer that I have a sickening feeling has already drowned.

It happens so fast. I've been in the water before with guys who died. Mark Foo at Maverick's. We were all laughing and joking with each other and then he caught a wave and just never came back to the lineup. We later found him down the rugged coast, floating with half his board still leashed to his ankle, dead. After that day, I lost my big wave motivation and never again heaved myself over the ledge of a three-story monster for the sheer thrilling joy of making a gigantic drop.

As I paddle in toward shore, I see the surfboard floating, fins up, just inside the impact zone. Rushing to his board, I roll off mine and grope down the leash toward the leg that I expect to still be attached. The turbulence and river silt make the water murky, but I grab his leg, push off the bottom, and with my one free arm swim to the surface. As the next wave sucks out, troughing around us, I take a split-second opportunity, plant my feet on the sand, and heave the surfer onto my board. There's a lot of blood and he's unconscious. I realize he's a grom, maybe fourteen or fifteen years old. I recognize him as one of the hot up-and-comers. A small wave breaks just behind us as I throw myself on top of his body and my board, and the wave pitches us toward the shore, gliding us onto the sand.

The guard from the nearby lifeguard stand must have seen the kid go down because he's already approaching, dropping his own rescue board, and running the final steps as I roll the body off my board onto the beach. The lifeguard checks for a pulse. He pushes a towel against the blood gushing from the boy's head. He starts CPR on the kid, clearing his mouth and pumping his chest. I recognize the familiar winter-surf sound of approaching sirens.

I figure there's nothing more I can do, so I turn around and paddle back out to catch another wave.

I try not to think about what happened. Whether or not the kid will live, or be OK, or whatever. As a pro surfer, I needed to stay convinced that we're all basically indestructible — even with firsthand evidence to the contrary. If I couldn't persuade myself into believing this little lie, I'd often be too terrified to surf.

As a young boy, I struggled with being afraid. Often left alone in my house, I worried about Nightmarchers, and almost anything else that could happen in the dark. Eventually, I stopped feeling paralyzed by fear, but the cost was to squish my feelings — all of them. By not allowing myself to feel afraid, I also stopped feeling other emotions, like goofy joy.

A girlfriend I thought I loved made me join her in a few couples counseling sessions because she couldn't understand how I wasn't enjoying my life, even though I had everything I imagined I ever wanted, including her. The counselor suggested that limiting my emotional range was a factor, and believed if I could allow myself to *feel* my fears and sadness again, then it would break open the high end, where joy and happiness were currently being held hostage.

In my defense, my feeling-smashing strategy allowed me to venture outside alone at night (which is sort of important when you're a teenager and want to go on a date), but I had to learn to ignore a lot of feelings, from terror to bliss. It was also my justification for smoking herb. Even though I didn't totally like the way it made me feel — sort of lazy and stupid-silly — I did like the way I simply forgot about anything that was bothering me. I stopped smoking, though, when I was in training, and I rarely smoked while I surfed competitively. I could feel it damaging my lungs, not to mention my attitude, which wasn't worth the trade-off of feeling temporarily at peace and not thinking about being scared. I also had a Kahuna share Ho'onoponopono with me when I was fourteen. Ho'onoponopono is an ancient Hawaiian practice of forgiveness that the Kahuna explained could help me get "pono," or right in the world, feel safe, and clean up any bad energy. He instructed me to repeat the chant, "I'm sorry, please forgive me, thank you, I love you," and direct it toward whatever or whomever caused me to feel afraid. I thought it sounded silly and that it couldn't possibly work, but since it seemed less damaging than weed, I tried it, and as if by magic, my fear slowly subsided. I must have whispered those words a thousand times and used the phrase as my go-to tool whenever I was afraid, or even angry or sad. For some reason, at this moment, I not only realize I haven't recited those words in years, but also that the power of the phrase existed primarily in my apologizing, forgiving, appreciating, and loving myself.

Right now, though, I just want to have a few beers after this session and stop thinking about what happened to that kid.

CHAPTER 3

KAIMANA

There's a beeping sound I recognize from police shows on TV that happens when a guy is shot and they're trying to get some crime-solving information out of him before he dies. I sniff a hint of alcohol, the kind I drip in my ears after surfing in dirty water.

I can't open my eyes, I can't budge my tongue or mouth to make a noise, and I can't move any part of my body in the slightest way. There is no pain. As I think about it, I have no sensation of my skin being in contact with anything: sand, water, or a bed. Am I home? On the beach? At the hospital? Could I be dead?

I'm only able to listen for short periods of time and then the noises and voices seem far away and blurred together. It feels similar to when I fight falling asleep when I have friends over and everyone's staying up super late; I strain to pay attention, to stay in the game, but then it's as if someone hits the "off" button and I'm out.

Sometimes I understand snippets. An unfamiliar man mumbles, "He's on day seven," which reminds me of a group of girls at school chatting about a cleansing diet they're all suffering through together. I'm alertly exhausted when I am able to hear things, concentrating and focusing as if I'm getting the instructions for the SATs after staying up late the night before. With growing desperation, I try to move any part of my body; I systematically start at the top of my head and urge something to stir, even an eyelash to flutter, but nothing responds.

I wonder what's broken. I push away thoughts that something truly awful has happened to me. What if I snapped my neck and I'm paralyzed, like that kid bodyboarding at Puka's? What if a shark attacked me and I'm missing body parts, like Bethany, but worse? My desperation morphs into the word "NO!" as my terrified, in-denial, overloaded brain shuts down and I go back to my dark, silent cave.

I hear my mom's ragged, sniffling breathing and she whispers, "Please, Kai" with far more desperation than when she's at her most frustrated trying to enlist me to do chores. I am guessing that her simple, pleading request is not a good sign. This tone of despair is coming from a woman whose tendency is to optimistically spin dire situations, like claiming we're probably avoiding an accident when we're stuck driving behind an absurdly slow tourist.

I hear my dad mumbling, but I don't understand what he's saying. His tone is the same one he uses for his pep talks before a surf contest, the "You can do it, you're better than these kids" speech, but the words are not about surfing, or about anyone else. He's trying to pump me up somehow, but for what?

I hear my little sister, bored and whining, asking the same questions over and over, "What's wrong with him? Why doesn't he get up?" She's five years old and a total pain, but I wish I could pull one of her braided pigtails so she'd try and punch me with her tangelo-sized fists. She's a whirling dervish made of flinging buggy-whip arms and legs when she attempts a retaliating assault on me or one of my friends.

What might be days later, I hear a woman say she's going to remove the staples from my head tomorrow, so it must be at least ten days since I was brought here. If I could move my arm, I would touch my scalp to count the small metallic strips. I've been hit in my head before with my board's fins, but I never needed more than four staples. Day ten of the coma diet. I wonder if this is how the saying "bored stiff" came about. My emotions run the gamut from apathetic disinterest to petrifying fear.

Mostly I realize that I want it to end — either I get up and go back to my life, or I stop having these little hearing-only awakenings. I can't stand being stuck inside myself, it's miserable and I'm totally over it. I hate being alone. This is worse than waking up in the middle of the night and hearing the last second of a strange noise, wondering if it was a dream, a catfight outside my window, or a murderer standing in my bedroom. My panic overrides curiosity and the blackness rolls back in.

CHAPTER 4

KEKOA

It doesn't matter how many beers I drink, I can't get the picture out of my head. It's not a snapshot of the kid unconscious and bleeding on the beach. Instead, I see a freeze-frame of the split second when he lurched forward. It was so unnatural. I've witnessed a million falls, but I've never seen a surfer riding a perfect, wide-open barrel get slugged in the back so hard that he got launched off his board and torpedoed forward, head first, arms tucked at his sides, like a superhero. In that moment, "that's weird" registered. Now, it's like my mind has taken a couple of burst-frame photos and won't put them away. What's bothering me is the look on his face right before he was heaved forward: the relaxed, easy set of his eyes and mouth, his poised posture, his whole being emitting pure satisfaction. He had no idea what hit him. He never suspected anything awful had happened to him. Part of me regrets dragging him to the shore. If he's going to die I should have left him in the ocean where he would have died happy, which is more than most of us can hope for.

My mind's photo of the second before his fall reminds me of that feeling of intense joy I used to safeguard after every surf session I had when I was growing up. It was a little package in my chest area that I could go back to anytime and revisit a surge of untainted contentment. It was different from conjuring up a memory. This package held volume and space in my body and waited patiently for me to retrieve it for my personal pleasure; it was accessible anytime I felt sad, mad, disappointed, or bored. It would stay with me for different lengths of time, sometimes an hour, or even days if it was a really good session.

Surfing meant everything to me; it was all I ever needed. It wasn't just the amazing feeling and sensation of the act of surfing, but it was also the lessons I learned on a board and how it shaped my life, taught me who I was becoming, and showed me how to find my place in the world. For most of my teen years, surfing was my religion and my guide.

I realize the expansive teaching I received from surfing has stopped, replaced by my ever-constricting reality. I don't feel I've learned anything new from surfing in years. During my last tutorial, I got my butt kicked on tour, packed up, and went home. The takeaway was, "I'm not good enough to compete at this level, so I should just quit and stop wasting everyone's time." The people who supported me — my sponsors and friends — were disappointed. Even my dad, who was too drunk most of the time to read the paper, left me a voice mail saying he was sorry the CT didn't work out. He never admitted it to me, but some of his Black Pot Beach drinking buddies told me he bragged about his "pro surfer" son. That's probably the only time I heard — directly or by rumor — about him being proud of me.

After work, while I aimlessly drive around looking for a place to grab a bite to eat, I find myself pulling into the hospital parking lot. Since I'm here, I figure I can check on that kid and see how he's doing. A day after the incident there was a blurb on a Kauai North Shore blog, which described the "surfing accident" and reported he was in a coma. The site updated the kid's status yesterday: still unconscious. It's been almost two weeks, which apparently doesn't offer much hope for a full recovery. The only mention of physical injury was a head wound, caused by a waterlogged coconut (which explains the sucker punch), which took twenty-eight staples to mend together.

When I get to the hospital, I ask for Kaimana Keller's room number but I'm told he's in the ICU and that only family members are allowed to visit. Undeterred, I take the elevator to the intensive care floor and see Kalli, a nurse I once dated, talking with the woman at the front desk.

I met Kalli in my late teens when she was a new ER nurse. Almost every serious surfer passes through the emergency room at one time or another. I've been treated five times at this particular ER, which is the only urgent care facility on Kauai. Those trips were for a broken collarbone (slammed on the sandbar), and staples (fin to the face, fin to the butt, and fin slices across both feet). I also visited the ER for a case of staph that went to my lymph nodes and sinuses and worried me more than the other injuries because, by the time I drove myself to the hospital, my body felt like it was totally shutting down. Kalli recognizes me and slides out from behind the desk to give me a limp hug.

"Hi, how's it going? Whatcha doin'?" she asks flirtatiously.

"Hey. I'm here to see the kid, Kai. He was brought in a few weeks ago."

"Oh." She pauses, and then says tersely, "He can't have visitors."

Realizing my social faux pas, I try a different tack; "Um, all right, how are things going for you? When did you switch to ICU?" I politely inquire.

"I left ER last year because I couldn't handle the daily onslaught of pain-med seekers. I swear, at least half the people coming in to the ER don't have real emergencies. Unless you count that they're out of OxyContin, or whatever pain med they're addicted to, which is apparently life or death for them. At least in the ICU the issues are real." She blurts that out in a way that helps me remember her; she was forthcoming with lots of information that I'm not sure I needed to hear.

In the interest of keeping her talking, I offer, "Yeah, I've heard some friends actually say they've gotten Percocet or other painkillers from ER by faking an injury. I used to think they were total losers for taking that stuff, but sometimes it seems like it might be an easier way to get through the days."

"Wow, I've never heard you sound so down. You're the golden boy. The self-made surf star. Rags to riches. That whole thing," she teases.

"Those days are gone. I'm just a half-assed carpenter trying to make a living so I can buy beer and maybe go on a surf trip once a year." I can hear the self-pity in my voice. It's embarrassing, but it's the truth. I feel sorry for myself. I had a miserable childhood, then a good run in my twenties, and now I have a used-up, boring, shitty life. Who wouldn't be bummed?

Regaining focus, I fib, "I'm actually a cousin of the kid's mom, and she suggested I stop by."

Her attitude and posture soften slightly. Taking a moment to consider an idea, she quietly says, "Come back in fifteen minutes. The intake nurse at the front desk has dinner break and I cover for her. I'll let you go back and take a look at him. He's totally unresponsive, though, so don't expect much." She then confirms that I'm not sick with anything, and also tells me to wash my hands with anti-bacterial soap before I come through the door.

Relieved, I offer, "Thanks. I'll go grab some coffee. Can I bring you a cup?"

Hastily, sounding like the last thing she needs is caffeine, she says, "Sure. That would be great. Two creams and four sugars, please."

I've always wondered why healthcare professionals don't take better care of their bodies. Some of them even smoke cigarettes. Maybe they see so many people with their lives destroyed due to uncontrollable outside forces that they figure it's all going to end anyway, so they might as well have a doughnut and a Red Bull, because at least for a few moments they'll feel hyper and tingly.

I come back fifteen minutes later with her coffee, and she reprimands me for bringing real sugar and little cream cups. Apparently, I was supposed to remember that she likes artificial sweetener and Coffee-mate nondairy creamer, which makes me even more curious about nurses' health choices. Nevertheless, she quietly beeps me through the front desk gate and points to Kai's room.

The machines attached to the kid drone out steady beeps. IV lines and electrodes emerge from multiple places on his body. His head is wrapped in gauze. He looks as small and fragile as an Akikiki finch; I remember one crashed into my bedroom window when I was six. Like the bird, the boy lies morbidly still. As I near the bed, I notice his light, shallow breaths.

I'm flooded with anger and I realize I'm pissed that this happened to him, especially while he was surfing. He probably thought he had it all going on, too. Then, in a nanosecond, it all changes. He may never come out of this coma. Even if he does, he'll probably be brain damaged or irreparably harmed. There's a part of me that thinks, "One less grom in the water" and I'm immediately consumed with guilt for conjuring up such a mean thought. It's not that I hate the groms. I don't even mind this particular kid. He loves to surf and he wore that passion on every ropey muscle in his agile body. I've felt his ocean-devotion in the previous times I've been in the lineup with him and I can see it in that mind-photo frozen in my memory. He has a symbiotic relationship with the sea; one of those wave-wizards, like Slater, that magnetically encourages the ocean to offer up her best waves when he's in the water.

I don't know why I stay. There's nothing I can do for the kid. I feel his alertness, though, his attention somehow directed at me even though he doesn't move in any way. His breathing doesn't sound like he's asleep. It's like he's patiently waiting. I might be imagining it, but it seems he's sniffing and concentrating, trying to figure something out. I silently sit, making a similar effort, and wonder, "Why him? Why me?"

CHAPTER 5

KAIMANA

Often I can tell who's in the room by his or her scent.

Hospital people smell like rubbing alcohol and the antibacterial hand soap at school.

My mom smells faintly like coconut and plumeria. It's the lotion she wears. One morning, running late for school, I couldn't find my Axe lotion, so I rubbed my mom's on my sunburned face, and the kids on the bus teased me all the way to school. When she's here, she holds my hand or massages my temples. She begs me to come back, prays to the universe for mercy, says affirmations for me like, "I'm strong, I'm healing, I'm waking up." Today I heard her offer herself up in my place. I never doubted her love for me, but the full force of that selfless dedication is now more apparent. I hate how awful this is for her.

My dad smells either like red dirt, cut grass, or his own coffee-infused sweat. He must stop by the hospital between his construction and landscaping jobs. He rarely speaks, but I know he's here. He puts his hand on my shoulder. It surprises me that he sits still so long, since he's usually very busy being busy. When he's here, I imagine he's trying to transmit his strength into me. It doesn't seem to help, but I appreciate his effort. I'm guessing he's mad at me for getting hurt while I was surfing. Both my parents surf and have always encouraged my surfing, but my dad probably thinks this happened because I'm a wimp. I'm sure he's upset and I'll probably get grounded for a month if I ever get out of here.

There's one person I can't identify. He must be a surfer because I can smell a faint scent of Carmex and Sticky Bumps wax. I know all the surf waxes by their fragrances — it's how I tell them apart when there's a pile of sandy wax chunks on the floor of my mom's truck. He also sometimes smells like freshly cut wood. He doesn't talk. He comes when no other people are here, and I can feel his presence. It's sort of a fuming, agitated energy. Like he's really disappointed in things, maybe in me. It reminds me of times when I knew my dad was mad and he didn't have to say anything. Usually I could tell by his facial expression, but now I realize I also knew by the way it feels to be around a person who's angry. With this guy, I can sense he's feeling upset and sort of defeated. I can't figure out why or how, but it's like he knows me. Not in the usual way, from school or cruising and talking, but more like when you meet someone new and feel as if you had already been thrown together in another place and time.

Apparently, the staples came out of my head today. Nothing seems to have changed. I'm scared being trapped inside my body. It reminds me of being buried up to my neck in beach sand by my friends. I yell and scream for help, for someone to see me, to scratch and dig the sand away, but no one hears, no one can save me.

I am panicked and feel helplessly resistant when hospital people come into the room. I envision them sticking needles into assorted places on my body, inserting a tube so I can pee, motioning my arms and legs, rolling me from one side to the other. I'm their Thanksgiving turkey and they're prepping me for roasting. It's a dull, painless, far-away prodding. Still, it's confusing and humiliating.

I'm causing my mom so much heartache. At home she can be snappy and demanding, but she does so much for me; brings me breakfast every morning by 6:15 so I can eat while I get ready to catch the bus, takes off early from work to pick me and my friends up from school to go surfing, films my sessions, and smiles encouragingly at me after every single contest heat — no matter how the heat went down.

My dad is probably super pissed at how much this is costing. He's worried about money; he's starting a new landscaping business and struggles with the island economy that's dependent on tourists. He's probably also upset that I got hurt surfing. He thinks that if I was more fit I wouldn't get hurt as often. He's always trying to convince and motivate me to workout with him — beach boot camp or lifting weights. I hate missing surf time for any of that stuff. Working out is difficult and boring, and I don't believe it improves my surfing. I think the only thing that trains a person for surfing is actual surfing; which is just another thing we disagree about. I know he loves me, but he's always disappointed in me. I've never quite been the son he wanted.

He was a baseball player, and he went to college on a baseball scholarship. When I was little, I played Little League and even made All-Stars my second year. I didn't want to go to Oahu for the championship series, which was the end of the world to him. I get As and Bs in school, but sometimes I get an "Unsatisfactory" for my behavior. My dad gets so pissed he threatens to sell all my surfboards. He went to an all-boys Catholic prep school and thinks he had it much tougher in high school than I do.

My dad may be right, at least academically; my mom is always telling friends on the mainland that the public schools in Hawaii are ranked the lowest in the nation, but I'm in the honors classes and there's a lot of other stuff to deal with than just schoolwork. I don't really know if I have any real friends. Some guys are fun to surf with but then act like jerks to me at school — like they're too cool to be seen with me out of the water. I don't fit clearly into any one group; I was born and raised here, I'm made up of about six different nationalities, and I have sun-bleached, brown hair and green eyes. Although I'm always tanned from surfing, I'm not as dark as the other local kids. I understand and speak pidgin easily, but the transplanted haole kids sound so dumb when they try to throw down some local talk that I try not to use the slang too much so I don't sound like them. I live on the North Shore, which is its own complicated world: it offers jaw-dropping beauty, some of it made by rains that never seem to end; at least five world-class surf breaks, each with its own set of local guys and rules to navigate; vacation homes of big-name celebrities and jet-setting bigwigs, and also a contingent of homeless people who camp at Anini and Haena Beach Park. I could buy pot or meth in any of the parking lots if I chose, and I could join my friends who, when they're bored, throw oranges and mud balls at tourists' cars. I take a school bus an hour each way to go to one of the two public high schools on the island. There's an expectation that since I'm from Hanalei I'm rich, but both my parents work, and I know they struggle to pay the bills. They drive ten- to fifteen-year-old trucks with rusted-out bumpers, and we never get to travel in first class or stay in the nice hotels when we go to other islands for contests. I'm not complaining. I have pretty much everything I need, and usually get three or four new surfboards a year, which is what's most important to me.

The scary thing is, it doesn't seem like there's any hope I'll ever be myself again or have that complex life with all those choices to consider.

If I'm paralyzed, I don't want to live. If I'm brain damaged, I don't want to live. If I can't ever surf again, I don't want to live.

I notice that each time I feel myself falling into the black pit of silent darkness, my expectation that I'll never wake up increases a tiny bit.

I feel completely alone and totally lost.

CHAPTER 6

KEKOA

Dammit! I screwed up another saw-cut. My mind keeps wandering, but my boss's yelling yanks me back to the present, "You're going to cut your hand off if you don't pay closer attention!"

I ask to take my lunch break early. He responds, "If you're going someplace to pull your head out of your butt, then sure, go ahead."

Since the jobsite is on Kauapea Road above Secret Beach, I kick off my workbooks, hike down the steep trail to third peak, pull off my sweat-soaked T-shirt, knock most of the sawdust off my board shorts, and jump in the ocean. Swimming straight out, I allow myself only ten breaths, and I look up to confirm I'm parallel with the lighthouse. It's one of my little tests to make sure I'm in the minimum shape necessary for solo surf sessions. If I pass this exam, then I can convince myself I have the basic cardio and swimming strength I need to surf alone at the outer reef breaks.

Unfortunately, I can plan on swimming in from a remote surf spot without a board at least once during a winter season. It usually follows a wild wipeout and a hold-down, too. While there's an abundance of wonderful feelings involved with surfing, one of those is not what you feel when your board pulls your leash to a taut tension and then you experience the snap, release, and sickening awareness that your leash has busted and your board has flung itself toward shore without you. Similar to a two-wave hold-down, those incidents taught me one thing: "let go." It's not giving up. It's not quitting. It's just letting go. I've heard my dad's AA pals say "Let go and let God." Surfers know this dictum intuitively. The ocean just happens to be the manifestation of God at that moment. To fight a wave that's holding you down is a complete waste of time and energy. Conceptually, this makes sense. To really "get it" though, you have to know what it feels like to intensely, desperately, and single-mindedly need a gulp of air. Nothing else. And instead of getting that air, you know you have to resist fulfilling that simple request from your body. Every cell of your being wants to fight and thrash your way up through the churning ocean to the surface, but you must relax, let go, and somehow find peace in that dark underwater place. You might be one foot or twenty feet down — there's no oxygen. Until the wave passes, you're not going anywhere else — except possibly to be drug along in the turbulence a little farther or deeper. I remember going to church with a friend when I was ten years old. The minister's sermon was titled, "This too shall pass." I was convinced the minister, who I assumed authored the saying, was a surfer.

Swimming back to shore, I decide I'll stop by the kid's hospital room again later today on my way home. I've gone a couple of times. It may not be helping him, but I notice I haven't been drinking beer as much in the evenings after I go to the hospital. During the days, even though my mind sometimes drifts when I'm at work, it has occurred to me that my job is not intrinsically terrible; it's somewhat intellectually challenging. I experience physical exertion (which helps keep my body strong), and I'm gratified when I complete projects. I'm outside some of the time and I have the freedom to take breaks, like this, to run down to the beach for a quick surf or swim.

Still, it's not the Championship Tour. I'm not a "surf star." Women aren't throwing themselves at me, like when I was on the CT. There's nothing left to strive toward. I spent my whole life, until eight years ago, aspiring to win the world title. Now, I don't compete at any level, and I rarely surf.

CHAPTER 7

KAIMANA

The guy I can't figure out is sitting next to me again. He may have been talking a few minutes ago. I haven't been listening to what people are saying. I don't want to hear my mom's sadness, my dad's anger, or the doctors mumbling about my vitals. I don't want to sense feelings in others. I pick up on their mood or attitude as they enter the room. It would be cool to have this skill in my other life, the one where I'm not a blob on a bed.

There's no hope, so why pay attention? I hate this world. It's too scary to try to understand what's happening with me. I can't believe I ever used to text my friend "FML." It was like I actually used to believe my life was so harsh, when all that might have happened was that some kid would be mean to me at school; or I was injured and couldn't surf for a few days; or one of my favorite video game disks was scratched; or I'd get one of my sinus infections that lasted more than a week. Any little thing could truly send me spinning into a place where I would actually believe my life sucked. I didn't know sucking before. Now my life truly sucks. FML.

CHAPTER 8

KEKOA

Kalli and I have worked out a routine. I show up when the ICU closes to visitors, minutes after the receptionist/guard takes her dinner break. Prior to my arrival, Kalli texts me things to bring (bribe) her. I arrive with the requested soda, gum, licorice, gossip magazines, and coffee (with fake cream and sugar). I supply her with unhealthy choices and she lets me sit by the kid.

He seems different tonight. The alertness, or his paying attention, that I thought I noticed before is gone. I wonder if he's dying and might not be here the next time I come by.

There's something that happens to me in this room, sitting next to a kid in a coma. My own life goes on hold and I'm thrown back to turning points.

Tonight, I'm reminded of a time when I was twelve and I signed up to surf in the NSSA contests. Only two of the eight contests took place on Kauai, the others were held on Maui, the Big Island, and Oahu. I had a little birthday money from my grandparents but my dad spent all his extra cash on booze. I tried to earn enough for airfare by climbing palm trees and cutting down coconuts to sell on the street, but I could barely get together enough money to pay the entrance fees.

Unexpectedly, one of the local surf shop owners, whose windows I sometimes wash in exchange for a new leash or deck pad, volunteered to pay my airfare to the NSSA contest at Sunset Beach on Oahu. When I arrived, the morning of the contest, the surf was pumping. I was entered in both Open Boys (twelve and under) and Open Juniors (thirteen-sixteen). The Open Boys heats are held at Vals, the inside break at Sunset. I made it to the finals and proudly took home a third place trophy. In the older boys' division, Open Juniors, the lifeguard, with Jet Ski patrol, permitted the heats to take place at the actual outside Sunset break. The ocean was wild. Surfline called it five-foot-plus Hawaiian, but there were bigger sets every ten to fifteen minutes and there was a ripping current dredging through the lineup.

One of the eighteen-year-old contestants from the Open Men's heat hysterically yelled at the contest director, "I got held down, pummeled, and almost drowned out there" at exactly the time I picked up my heat jersey from the tent. I was thoroughly terrified to paddle out for my heat.

I also knew the boys in my heat were up to four years older than I was, more experienced, better surfers, and far stronger overall. I'd surfed big waves on Kauai — The Bay at over five feet, Majors, even bigger. But both are perfect point breaks and I'd surfed those spots at all sizes and in all conditions. I knew the channel, the current, the reef, and the part of the wave where it's not advised to fall.

I had never surfed Sunset. My fearful mental spinning paused so I could hear the contest director squawk over the speakers, "Five minutes, five minutes. Next heat you can paddle out." I'd only competed in beach starts before, but I was instructed at check-in that morning that since the break is more than a hundred yards out in the ocean that each heat would be given five extra minutes to make it out closer to the lineup. I was also informed that standing up on my board, before the third horn blows between heats, signaling the start of my heat would result in an interference or disqualification call.

As I hesitantly jogged down the beach to paddle out with the other, larger boys, I noticed a man trotting along beside me. Breathing loudly between sentences, he said, "Hi, Kekoa, I'm Mike from Quiksilver. We heard about you from a couple of our friends on Kauai and we've been watching you surf today. We're impressed. After your heat I'd like to talk with you and your parents about sponsoring you."

My debilitating fear was suddenly replaced by a new awareness, an amazing thought — someone thought I was good enough to sponsor. I didn't respond to the man, but I sprinted the rest of the way down the beach, paddled out with the big boys, and when the horn blew to start my heat, my chest was puffed up as if I had gained ten pounds of muscle.

Paddling into my first wave, I was immediately pitched, straight off a heaving lip. Plunging head first, unable to push my board away from me, dragging along the ocean bottom, prone on my board, I popped up directly in the bull's-eye of the impact zone. I wasn't flooded with embarrassment and fear and I didn't dwell for a second on my clear kook-ness, but instead I paddled with all the little muscles in my eighty-pound body right back to the center of the lineup. One of my fellow competitors, with just a touch of concern, asked if I was okay. Another ordered me to go sit on the shoulder and get out of the way. I paddled around, in and out, watching the other guys ride waves, and finally put myself in position to possibly catch one in the next flurry. As the following set rolled in, I was out deeper than the others and in the spot to catch the first wave. When I quickly switched from sitting to lying on my board, so I could paddle for the wave, I felt the tail of my board jolt hard to the left, throwing me out of position and placing the surfer next to me in the takeoff spot. I later learned that little kick-action is called the "NSSA push," and that kids do it to each other to move another surfer out of the way so they can catch the wave instead. I couldn't even imagine that a competitor would do that to another surfer, so the only possible explanation I could come up with at the time, was that a shark must have bumped me, because nothing had ever knocked my board that firmly. I didn't have time to panic though; the next wave was lurching up directly in front of me. I knew I was a little too deep, but I desperately wanted to get away from the "shark," so I spun, paddled, and somehow caught the wave. I got to my feet clumsily as the white water of the lip bounced and lurched me, but I managed to stay upright and make a couple of big, sweeping turns on the open face. Once I was surfing, the fear and self-doubt rinsed off me like back spray. I found my rhythm, felt my feet on my board, and saw the wave shaping up in front of me in slow motion as I pulled in neatly to a tight tube on the inside and got spit out not far from shore. I heard whoops and yells from the beach. My inner voice cheered, "I did it. I rode a massive wave at Sunset! I even got a barrel!" I was stoked, proud, and absolutely giddy with happiness.

I didn't catch another wave in that heat, and I didn't make the cut due to only one wave score, but I emerged from that heat transformed. Two people believed in me; the rep from Quiksilver and myself.

Suddenly, it dawns on me that I've been talking aloud. I look at the kid. He's still far, far away and looks more and more like the broken bird every time I see him.

CHAPTER 9

KAIMANA

I enjoy listening to the space inside my head. There's a dark screen on which I watch short movies of my life. I take comfort in replaying memories, like when I received my first brand-new, shaped-for-me surfboard on Christmas morning. The firm, glassy smooth way it felt under my arm, how sick the red-and-blue flames looked. Or when my new puppy, Tickster, nipped at my toes and made squeaky yips while we rolled around together on the sloping lawn. Or the time my mom was driving me to school and I made her laugh so hard that coffee squirted out her nose and she swerved to the side of the road because she couldn't see. For years, repeating one line from that conversation could get her to crack a smile, even when she was fuming mad at me. Or, there was an evening my dad and I played catch in our yard until past sunset. After we could barely see each other, I threw my first curve ball, finally getting the spin and speed just right, and the ball slapped straight into the pocket of my dad's glove. I replay that whoosh-smack sound over and over.

I don't want to hear what's going on outside of me. I don't want to pay attention. I don't want to feel what other people are feeling now — it's all bad. There are no good feelings, not even any medium ones — just awful, sad, angry, desperate, giving-up feelings.

Somehow, seeping through the crevices in the rock wall I've built around myself, I hear the surfer recalling a story, and I can sense a different energy from what the other people who come and go from this room have been emitting. It's not directed toward me, like everyone else's is. He even seems caught off guard by this attitude, as if he thought he'd never feel it again. It's sort of like how I felt about being assigned lab partners with the new girl, a glimmer of something unexpectedly possible. His energy is usually heavy, but for the first time it's not uncomfortable to have him near.

CHAPTER 10

KEKOA

The phone text from my boss reads, "no work till 10 … drywall guys finishing up." Knowing I have three extra hours this morning feels like a gift. I figure I should clean up around my little cottage and maybe do some laundry, but instead I grab my board, run down the dirt road, across the two-lane, twenty-five-mph highway, through some rich guy's vacant, unused, multimillion-dollar beachfront lot, down the sand a hundred yards, and paddle out to Tunnels.

Even though it's winter, the water's a warm seventy-eight degrees and there's surprisingly light wind, so I trunk it and find that I'm the only surfer beyond the reef at dawn, which is amazing. It's not big, by Haena standards, but it's another NW swell, and it's hitting the reef at the direction I prefer. Between sets, I catch sight of a whale breaching near the horizon, throwing spray higher than one of Pancho's hacks at Backdoor. Next to me, a glistening turtle head pops up less than a board's length away; with watery, old-man-eyes, he slowly rotates his head to surmise if I'm edible. The sun is floating upward above the St. Regis with the current crop of celebrities asleep in their four thousand-dollar-a-night suites. At this moment, I wouldn't trade places with any of them. There's a rightness I haven't felt since before I went on the QS, a certainty that there's no difference between me and the ocean, the whale, the turtle, and J. Lo's latest boyfriend.

I first realized this notion when I was about fourteen. I had fallen on a late drop and was getting pummeled by a wave at Flatrock. While being drug underwater a hundred feet along the reef, I opened my eyes — mostly to try and dodge my board or the reef — and I noticed a monk seal traveling the same journey alongside me. We both weighed about a hundred pounds, and my black spring suit resembled sealskin, but when I saw the seal gleefully accepting the "Bay drag," two things occurred to me:
#1. We're all in this together, and
#2. It's fun if you let it be.

Until that time, I had taken on my dad's attitude of "f**kin' tourists, longboarders, slow drivers, gays, haoles, holy rollers, hippies, and county workers." It worked for me because it made me feel better than all of "those" people and allowed me to believe for a second, on some level at least, that I had my life more together than they did. Something about the seal's playful glance in my direction shattered that long-held philosophy. I realized in my cells that I had something in common with a seal. What might I have in common with walking-on-land mammals that just happen to look or act different from me? And, if getting bounced along a reef could be enjoyable, how much fun was I missing moving around on dry land, where I had air in my lungs and full use of my limbs?

Unexpectedly, a rogue wave rolls through, knocking me off my board, and the shock of water on my dry head prompts me to think about the kid in the coma. I wonder what he believes, what he's already decided about life and himself. Mostly I wonder if he'll ever get the opportunity to really figure stuff out; to have a chance to test his theories; to see what works and what doesn't for him in his unique life.

After my surf, and another text from my boss delaying my arrival at work again, I still have two hours before I need to be at the jobsite, so I drop by the hospital to check on the kid. It's not my usual visiting time, but I luck out because the doctors are on their rounds through ICU. The guard nurse is away from her post, so I slide through the ajar security door and into Kai's room. I hear the approaching doctors turn the corner at the end of Kai's hall, working their way toward us, and realize I have only a few minutes.

Making physical contact with Kai for the first time, I reach out and give his curled-up, pale hand a little knuckle bump and say, "Life doesn't just happen to you, it's a choice you make — every day, every hour, every minute."

CHAPTER 11

KAIMANA

I'm breathing underwater, weightlessly gliding with the current, gently bouncing along the bottom of the ocean. A school of ahi executes synchronized swimming maneuvers more gracefully than Olympic competitors. Spinner dolphins roll five feet below me, then with one whip of their tails, rocket toward the surface and launch ten-point airs, one flinging a leaf up and catching it on his nose as both splash back in the water. The sunlight beckons above me but I have no desire to leave the spacious sea cradling and embracing me. I see visible lines, like mist off the back of a breaking wave, connecting me to all the creatures in the ocean and on land. I feel grateful for all I've experienced, for everyone who's loved me, for each delicious piece of food I've eaten, for every wave I've ever surfed. I'm falling and floating and disconnecting. Attachments, to people, places, and stuff, have lost interest with me. I'm blissfully satisfied, alone and with nothing. It's just like being inside a perfect barrel.

Something bumps against my hand, and like a hooked fish, I struggle against coming up from the depths of my ocean.

CHAPTER 12

KEKOA

Darting past the still-empty nurse's station, as the touring doctors enter the adjoining room to Kai's, I make a date with myself to return this evening.

It's clear the kid is dying. His life force is flowing out of him like a draining low tide. I console myself knowing there's nothing I can do to help him — I'm certain his family and the medical staff have done everything possible.

Ruminating about the life Kai will never get to experience while hustling to make it to work on time, I jerk my steering wheel sharply as a wandering dog lazily weaves out of the bike lane onto the highway. Jarred back to the present by the dog's painful yelp, I pull over, grudgingly jump down from my truck, and embark on a halfhearted search for the dead or injured animal. There's no carcass on the road. Imagining he's crawled into the tall grasses, I push through the weeds, gently whistling to him. Following a disjointed blood trail, I find a small poi dog, curled up on the ground, steadily licking his squished tail and hind leg. "Oh, buddy," I murmur, "I'm so sorry." Without missing a lick, his accusation-less eyes lock on mine. Stripping off my flannel shirt, I fashion some sloppy protective gloves and reach out, hoping he'll allow me to pick him up. His lips curl under, and his jumbled teeth flash at me as he emits a deep, guttural growl from the back of his throat.

I am not a dog person. I did not own a dog as a kid. My dad said they were a hassle and cost too much, but one of my friends had a Jack Russell terrier named Shadow (because when he got the puppy, the boy wanted him to follow him everywhere). This injured dog looks like a long lost cousin of that pooch. Shadow was the coolest dog ever — he surfed on the nose of a long board, executed flawless flips if you kicked sand over his head, dug up sand crabs and dismantled them leg by leg, and swam the breaststroke underwater while he chased fish. He was lean and muscular — twenty-five pounds of hairy athleticism. He hung out with us kids on the beach while we surfed for hours, amusing himself and dozens of passing tourists with his antics. When I returned to the beach for a snack, or to re-wax my board, I remember teasing Shadow, trying to pull away a stick he was gnawing on, or giving him a bit of my lunch and then acting like I was taking it back. Shadow had the same snarl as this mutt — a really menacing "big-dog" face and growl. The thing was, Shadow never bit me. He'd put up a show, but I could take food, or even a sand crab missing two legs, right out of his mouth, and he'd do the guard dog act right up until the second I thought he'd dig his teeth into my hand. Then he would just sort of hum out the end of a growl like a fade-to-black in a rock song. I'm hoping there's enough Shadow in this mutt to produce the same level of actor-singer, as I continue to reach toward him even though he's snarling and fiercely growling. I wrap him in my shirt, keeping my hands away from his injury, and gingerly, stiffly follow my original trail back to my truck. His growl becomes more like a gargling sound and he's focused on his self-help licking as I place him in the front seat next to me and pull back into traffic with a jittery level of alertness. I'm late for my job, but I feel content with my actions, and I'm hoping the homeowner I work for is taking her usual day off and will be able to examine my injured captive.

Luckily, I see Dr. Jenna gracefully sliding into her car as I drive my truck up the curved, crushed-coral driveway to her home and my jobsite. Having never said more than a professional "Aloha" prior, I gather up my courage, throw my door open, and rush to catch her door before she can close herself into her vacuum-sealed Volvo.

"Um, excuse me, sorry to startle you, there's an injured dog in my truck and I wonder if you could take a look at him and maybe see if he needs to be put to sleep?" I burst out in one breath.

Taking a second to recognize I'm one of the guys who has toiled daily on her home for the past three months, she composes herself, slides past me on her way to the passenger door of my truck, and quietly asks, "Is it your dog?"

"No. I hit him. Not on purpose, of course. He wandered into the road and I clipped him, I guess, with my front truck tire — I didn't see him. I was daydreaming sort of, and I wasn't paying attention," I blabber.

She opens the door as a couple of empty Java Kai to-go coffee cups fall on her slippered feet and without commenting, firmly scratches the licking dog behind his ear. "How you doing, sweetie?" she asks compassionately.

"Oh, I'm doing okay, sort of upset about hitting the dog," I reply.

"I am speaking to the dog," she lightly informs me.

What is wrong with me? I am a bumbling fool, but I pull it together enough to mutter, "Right, of course — is he going to die?"

"First of all, he's a she. Secondly, yes, she'll die eventually, as all living things do, but not likely from these injuries. She needs to be cleaned up and she might lose a section of her tail, but her leg doesn't appear broken and the bleeding has stopped." She turns, crisply walks past me toward her house, and returns with a hastily thrown together tray of medical supplies.

She then instructs me, "Instead of moving her, I'd like you to sit on the floor of your truck and scratch her head to distract her while I clean her wounds and assess the damage."

Luckily, I'm flexible, and by sliding the front passenger seat back, I can just barely cram myself between the dash and seat, which I do without questioning the lovely doctor, even though it puts my face right at eye level with the now-growling-again dog.

Dr. Jenna informs me, "Your job is to keep her head facing forward so she can't see what I'm doing. It's going to hurt her a little and she'll try to get away from you, but if you place your hands behind her head and scratch the back of her ears, you should be able to keep her from biting you, and me. Oh, and it helps if you keep a running dialogue going with her."

"Don't you mean a monologue?" I ask.

"No, I mean a dialogue — you talk to her, she talks back, you talk to her, etc. It's a conversation: I'm hoping you've engaged in those before?" she asks with a slight hint of sarcasm.

I'm not really sure how to have a two-way communication with a dog, but given the contribution Dr. Jenna is making to the process, I figure I can try to do my part as requested.

I place my hands gently around the dog's small head and scratch her ears as she casually drops her weight into my hands, slightly rolling onto her side with the injured leg up.

"Good. Now start talking," the veterinarian encourages.

"So, little doggie, how is your day going? Oh crap, that's a poorly chosen question." I take back.

The vet quickly cleans the cuts and wraps the dog's bent tail. She moves the dog's leg at the knee joint, which seems to move without causing pain. The dog is pulling backwards on my hands and is trying to twist free to examine the smaller hands on her hindquarters. Dr. Jenna glances over her glasses and requests, "Will you please talk to the dog? I don't have any Novocain and I need you to keep her distracted."

Recalling the only dog memory I can quickly access, I ask, "Catch any crabs or fish lately? Hang ten on any longboards? Do any back flips?"

Both the dog and Dr. Jenna stare at me with quizzical faces. The vet recovers quickly and returns to her work, cleaning and taping. The dog raptly hangs on my every word. Since I can't think of additional antics of Shadow's, I keep rambling, mixing it up a bit, "Catch any surfers being kooks? Flip off any bad drivers?"

Since I'm embarrassing myself, I look intently into the dog's eyes, trying to keep her attention on me. I can see recognition in the way she swivels her ears, and then I remember that Shadow had a vocabulary of something like a hundred words. "Beeeeeaaaachhhhhh?" I ask, elongating the word into two syllables, like we used to do to playfully torment Shadow when home. The pup's head turns, and she replies, "uuuhhhnnnneee" and intently gazes at me, waiting for another word she loves.

"That … is dialogue," Dr. Jenna commends. "And, I'm finished. She's good to go."

Thanking the doctor, I roll the windows down in my truck and move it to a shady spot where I'm hoping the dog will sleep while I put in my half-day's work. I inform the pooch I'll take her to the Humane Society later. She doesn't have on a collar, but maybe she's lost and being missed by some little kid right now.

After work, though, like a mislabeled letter going back to sender, I instead return to the hospital parking lot.

CHAPTER 13

KAIMANA

The only voice I hear, the only scent I smell, and the only person I hesitantly return to the surface for is the stranger. He doesn't judge me, need me to get better, pity me, or expect anything from me. His presence reluctantly magnetizes my attention as I'm pulled into his shifting energy. Like pushing up from a long hold-down, I suspect he's becoming lighter and seeing more clearly as he approaches the boundary between the water and air. In the beginning, he wore his anger and disappointment like my old Iron's Brothers Contest T-shirt, stained and thinning but still serving a purpose. His heaviness is fading, becoming replaced with a feeling that reminds me of being awoken in the middle of the night by the thunderous vibration of pounding surf — and knowing in my dreamy sleep state that a new swell is arriving.

CHAPTER 14

KEKOA

No one is searching for this dog through the SPCA. The clerk said I could leave her at the Humane Society kennels, or keep her until the owner came to claim her. The dog needs me to clean her wounds and re-tape her tail, like the gorgeous Dr. Jenna showed me, which I figure is the least I can do since I'm the reason she's injured. I posted on Craig's List and Facebook, and put signs on the bulletin boards at Foodland and Java Kai, so her owners will probably call to retrieve her any day.

In the meantime, she spends every waking minute by my side, and sleeps in my truck's passenger seat while I'm working. She's a comical little creature who continuously amuses me. When she walks, she has a hitch in her gait and she pulls in her injured leg every third step. Her tail resembles an "L," and the vet said it will remain that way if it heals, but it may have to be removed below the crushed tip. To aid in her mending process, I take her to a few of my favorite beaches and have temporarily named her Shadie, my interpretation of the female version of the name Shadow. Like Shadow, she's clearly a hunter; I've already removed a squawking chicken, four fumbling sand crabs, and a thrashing papio from her mouth. The chicken and fish escaped intact but the sand crabs are each missing a few legs. Unlike Shadow, she doesn't jump directly on any surfboard that happens to be lying on the beach, or going or coming from the water. I plan to borrow a longboard from a neighbor and take her for a paddle inside the reef. I recall a time at Makaha, when I asked Rell Sunn if Shane (one of her many dogs), who often perched on the nose of her nine-foot board, enjoyed surfing with her. She shrugged and said, "Dogs go out once, and from that point on, they know they're different. Shane surfs, canoes, and rides on the front of my board. After the session, he kind of crosses his legs on the porch, looks at the other dogs, and he's like, 'Yeah … riff-raff.' All animals are that way. From the time they get on that board, they know they're special. Brian Keaulana took a pig out once. The pig acted differently from that day on, and went back to the farm with an attitude." Not that Shadie lacks confidence, but I've always felt surfing heals the soul, and, well, if it can repair at that level, it might fix a broken tail.

Parking my truck under a shade tree at the hospital, I pour a fresh bowl of water and offer a new squeaky toy to Shadie. Uninterested, she pounces over to my empty driver's seat, and as I'm walking away she bangs out a tempo with her front paws on the inside of the half-open window.

Enticed back to the truck, I ask, "What's the matter, girl? You just peed, and you wait for me in the truck all the time, what's up?"

"Ummmm, eeeeee, ahhhhhhh," she responds from the back of her throat, sounding a bit like a miniature donkey.

Shadie is quite the conversationalist, but she's more efficient at understanding me than I her. Shadie's body language is sometimes easier to translate than her words, and I notice she's dropped her paws from the window to the door armrest and is tapping her front paw on the electric window button. When we're driving, she's figured out that this action allows her to lower the window and rest her chin on the side mirror, which balloons her lips at speeds over thirty mph. She's smart, but she hasn't figured out that the window button works only when the truck is running. I can't help chuckling as I reach through the partially open window, turn on the ignition, and lower the window for her.

Assuming I've solved her problem, I turn again to walk away, but she's still humming noises through her closed lips as she lurches out the window, jumps onto my shoulder, and clings to me like a parrot. Her sheer athletic ability and balance awes me, not to mention her will to get her way, so I return to the truck, dump out a backpack full of leashes, fins, wax and duct tape, and place her inside. She happily curls herself into the exact shape of the pack and does not make a peep when I zip it closed. I'm pretty sure animals aren't allowed in ICU, but I'm willing to risk increasing my anticipated "hospital criminal charges" and remind Shadie, "No talking," as we walk through the lobby and into the Intensive Care Unit. I hand Kalli today's high-sugar-but-fat-free bribes and walk into Kai's room.

Shadie sits statuesquely and quietly on my lap and I reward her by scratching her favorite soft spots. Seeing her grasp of proper ICU behavior, I raise her over the stainless steel bar and gently place her on Kai's bed. She tenderly snuggles under his arm for the rest of her nap. Knowing she understands English, I tell her about the first time I surfed big Middles in Hanalei Bay.

"So, Shadie, I'm about fifteen years old. I'm fairly sure my dad is hanging out at Black Pot getting pickled, so I avoid The Bay because if I go there after he's been drinking, he yells mean things at me, like 'Hey, hot-shot surfer boy, still afraid of the dark? Still cry every time you get a little boo-boo?' causing all the other drunks to laugh and make fun of me as I walk by to surf.

"What I didn't understand until much later in life was that my dad's flipping out on me whenever I was afraid or showed emotion when I got hurt was really his hatred of his own fears and vulnerabilities. Drinking was his way of dealing with the pain he felt because my mom left him when I was little. It made him forget, at least temporarily, how sad and broken he felt. His family raised him to never cry, and instilled the belief that boys are sissies if they showed any emotions other than bravado or anger. I hated my dad for not caring about me, or trying to understand that I was different from him, and I envied other boys whose dads showed them compassion or kindness.

"Once, when I was in my twenties, I confronted my dad, having concluded it was his fault that I drank and smoked pot to try and squelch my feelings since I had no other way to deal with them. My dad's response was that he was using 'tough love' to raise me to be a man. 'Funny thing,' I told him, 'I don't remember any love, just tough.'

"I've grown to feel sorry for him, seeing how he won't allow himself to express his lifetime of pent-up pain, because then he'd be a sissy in his eyes. He's the only parent I ever had, so I needed him when I was growing up to provide me a place to live and food to eat. I desperately wanted him to love me, which made me try all the time to be the kid he wanted me to be: tough, strong, impervious to pain, and a winner. I aimed to live up to my name, which means 'The Brave One' in Hawaiian. My mom named me, and then she left us. I believe she knew from the start that I wasn't courageous, and that I needed a namesake to help me overcome that character flaw. Through surfing, I learned that pretending to be brave has it drawbacks.

"Knowing I need to hone my backside for the upcoming Regional Championships at Kewalos and State Championships at Alamoana Bowls, my personal training program is to surf Middles, one of the juicier hollow lefts in the bay, as often as it's breaking. On this particular day, there is a solid, five-foot NE swell and light sea winds that blow up the face of Middles and create a gaping, fast barrel. I'm about five-and-a-half feet tall, so the face of the wave is easily twice as big as I am, and Middles is known for dredging out under sea level, as it sucks up on the reef in the center of the bay.

"As I approach the break, after a long paddle out through a churning, river-rushed channel, I count at least twenty guys in the lineup. It's bigger and meaner than I expected, which is often the case out here. This break sends many surfers packing back to the beach after one wave, or more often, after one wipeout. I'm scared, but I'm forcing myself to override my gut feeling of terror with thoughts like, 'the only thing to fear is fear itself.' I heard that in my history class and it pretty much summed up my dad's rambling, slurred lectures to me about how I shouldn't be a wimp, how I should suck it up, act tough, and, at all costs, never look like a pansy.

"Swallowing the acid that's bubbling up the back of my throat, I paddle deep into the lineup with the expert surfers; guys who have manhandled this wave for years. A few offer me nods of acknowledgement, but most paddle deeper and farther away from me so they won't have to assume responsibility for my well-being, which they know is at risk given the size and direction of this swell.

"The outside reef — Queens — feathers, which signals an approaching massive set. Like a flock of Nene turning toward their nests, all the surfers pivot and stroke directly at the approaching wall of water. As I scramble up the face of a fluid, twelve foot face with no back, I understand in my cells what Gerry Lopez meant when he said, 'the horizon goes black,' when he was talking about surfing second-reef Pipeline on a huge swell. There's a wave coming at us that's twice the size of the previous one, which I barely scratched my way over. It's a snake-green, frothing sky-rise coming toward us on a tsunami. My stomach cramps in a sensation I can only imagine is what an appendix rupturing might feel like. I realize there's zero chance I'll be able to paddle over this monster. It's physically impossible for me to duck-dive anything this huge, and as the wave starts to throw, I gauge my current trajectory and the wave's pitch and decide it will place me exactly in the impact zone of an open-ocean eight-footer.

"I determinedly attempt a duck-dive, hoping to at least get deeper and further out than the pitching lip, but unfortunately, as I imagined, my body is directly under the downward heaving, fastest-moving part of the wave. It implodes on my legs, smashing them into my board with enough velocity to drive my knees through the resin, sharply into the severed deck. My board is ripped from my hands and I'm driven twenty feet down into the black depths of the reefy ocean floor. As I tumble, trying to curl into a protective ball, the tension pulls my hands and feet in opposite directions, and I feel escalating panic as I realize that the deep breath of air I gulped before piercing the wave has been punched out of my lungs. I force myself to accept the 'letting-go,' Zen-like state of calm, trusting the ocean will ultimately give me up.

"Eventually I pop to the surface, with time to grasp a short breath and dive down again as another wave explodes ten feet outside of me. I dive below the driving, frothing foam to the clear, dark water deep below. Dealing with the remaining five set waves in the same manner, I'm callously pushed a hundred yards inside where I finally get a respite from the onslaught. Assessing my situation, I take a quick inventory; my board is gone — the leash must have snapped because three feet of cord dangles from my leg; my head is pounding, but I can't find any gashes, just a growing bump on my forehead; both legs are cut and bleeding above and below my knees where they penetrated my board; I have a searing, knife-hot pain in my shoulder, and when I reach up to rub it through my wetsuit top; there seems to be a ledge between my collar bone and the round part of my shoulder; the worst piece of news — I can't seem to make my right arm stroke so I can swim to shore.

"If ever I should be throwing a tantrum, it would be now, but instead of feeling shame like when I cry in front of my exploding dad for some minor injury, I let the tears roll down my cheeks and allow myself to be sad for what's happened to me: how I've wrecked my body and lost my only big wave board. I don't feel guilty or sissy-like; I know this is just what's true. I'm hurt, I'm sad, I'm crying, and I'm swimming myself to shore with one arm and some really messed-up legs. It takes about a half hour for me to get to the beach, and then I have to walk another quarter mile to the parking lot. Halfway there, the lifeguard from Retro's, who must have spied me with his binoculars, intersects my path. The guard is a known waterman and without accusation, says, 'Looks like the wave got the better of you today. Wanna come over to the guard stand so I can make sure you're good to go?' Dazed, but thinking clearly enough to know I need help, I follow him to his watchtower. Without taking off my wetsuit top, he gently turns my back to his chest, takes my bicep in one hand and placing his other on top of my collarbone, he firmly pops the ball of my shoulder back into the socket, informing me it was dislocated. The searing pain immediately stops. He asks me to sit on the nearby picnic table and brings over his first-aid kit, gently pulling fragments of surfboard glass from my legs and pouring hydrogen peroxide, then Betadine, liberally over both sets of sliced quads and shins.

"He asks for my parents' phone number and says he'll call them to take me to the ER. I know my dad's unreachable, we don't have insurance, and he'll just say I need to toughen up. I softly plead to the lifeguard, 'Can you just fix my legs like you did my shoulder?' He admits, 'I shouldn't of actually set your shoulder, as there are limits to what lifeguards are legally allowed to do, but I could tell you were in pain and I didn't want you to have to wait for the paramedics.' He shows me how to clean my leg wounds, butterflies, and tapes them closed, and tells me to stay out of the water for a few days and to frequently clean the cuts.

"Unexpectedly, I see my surfboard leaning against a leg of the guard stand and mutter, 'That's my board, how did it get here?' While I hold an ice pack on my lumpy forehead, the guard replies, 'A tourist walking The Bay brought it over and asked if maybe there shouldn't be a person attached to it.' It's what alerted me to turn my focus from the beach-breaks to farther out in the bay. I figured the down-surfer couldn't be too big if he's riding a six-foot board today out at Middles — it's triple overhead.' Wondering if I should apologize to him for going out there, I instead say, 'Actually, it's my step-up, my regular shortboard is five foot five' He hands me his bottle of water and says, 'Y'know, it's okay to know your limits. We all learn, in our own way, what we are and aren't capable of; and it changes, over time, in different directions. There's a voice inside you that will tell you whether or not to go out, and it's critical you only listen to your own inner voice and no one else's.' I think about the voice that told me I had 'nothing to fear but fear itself' and realize it's my dad's words overriding my own. I knew, earlier today, I was out of my league at that break. I recall another voice, as I lopsidedly swim to shore, encouraging 'you're okay, you're alive, just get to the beach.' That voice didn't care if I was crying and struggling. It supported me even though I had my ass handed to me on a platter. At thirty-three years old, I realize something I didn't then — I was crying from more than just the pain from my injuries and the loss of my board; I was afraid, I was hurt, and like the Hokualea, I was completely alone finding my way through the massive, impersonal ocean without any navigational tools."

CHAPTER 15

KAIMANA

The sound resembles a strange combination of snoring, purring, and gargling. It's sweetly alluring, and I think of land animals instead of my usual aquatic companions who mesmerize my days and nights. I love my under-the-surface world, yet I'm curiously drawn to understand what this creature is whose vibrating warmth I sense at my side.

I resist being pulled above the ocean, but I hear the stranger telling another surfing story, and I weakly fight my amphibian-self's resistance, shake the water from my ears, and turn my focus to his words.

Settling into the deeper message within his monologues and the flow of his shifting energy, it reminds me of skateboarding on my half-pipe when I was seven years old and an older friend telling me to "go with the board" while I rotated off the coping. I initially resisted, as I instinctively wanted to spin the board with my hand and keep my body facing forward, but eventually I tried my nine-year-old mentor's suggestion. After I fell dozens of times and scraped my knees and elbows enough to warrant purchasing pro-style pads, I finally executed a full rotation flawlessly. The real payoff, though, happened a few years later when my body and brain easily grasped how to do air reverses while surfing.

It's simply a willingness to skate through whatever shows up and trust that it's all contributing.

This guy has had a lot of shit happen in his life. He's had a hard time with his family. He hasn't had support. He's got issues he's had to deal with, like his fear. We're different, but there is something in his words that resonates with me, like two dissident notes in a guitar chord.

Along with our connection, I am aware of his aloneness, of my separateness. We are each free-falling shooting stars. To some, our presence is a brief "Ooooohhh," perhaps something they accidentally spied while taking out the garbage on a cloudless night. To others, who are watching and waiting for our path through the sky, it's a lifetime of attention. It doesn't matter, because whether people are critiquing or not, it's not their life to judge; his life is his, and my life is mine.

Catch and release — just like fly-fishing in the stream by my house — means I unhook from the burden of others' expectations, needs, and desires. I let go. It's not that I give up or quit, it's just that I relinquish my need to control and concede my own hopes, surrendering to whatever the ocean of my life chooses to do with me. I accept my destiny with open arms.

In this moment, everything is right. I have a peaceful, satisfied sensation inside me. I'm full of completeness, of being enough. As I allow myself to intensely feel this contentment, I think of other times I've felt this pleasure.

The obvious experiences have occurred surfing; putting together a solid heat, landing an air, or being spit out of a barrel. But there are other times that float into my awareness, rolling back in time, and the sensations flood through my body as if those things are happening now. Things like calming my upset little sister so that her body relaxes into sleep against my chest; spying Hanalei Bay spilling out thousands of feet below me after a solo hike to the top of Hihimanu; sliding, exhausted, into cool, clean, crisp sheets; placing a young, frightened girl in her father's trembling arms after plucking her from a rip; burying sobs in my mom's soft shoulder while she carries me two blocks home after I did a face-plant on my first skateboard ride to check the surf; hearing my dad tell me he loves me, through my self-hatred, after striking out in Little League championships; and cradling my bouncy, lick-crazed puppy in the car when we took him home to be ours forever all come into view. I am aware of deep gratitude, of being abundantly thankful, of feeling chosen to have the coolest, most incredibly fantastic life. How did I not notice that when I was out there having it? What kept me from seeing, all the time, every minute, that my life was amazing? I wasn't sad or depressed; I just wasn't satisfied. I didn't grasp that my puppy's milky kisses were enough. Because if I could have just allowed myself to feel those licks, the scratchy, slippery warmth of his nuzzle and tongue on my neck, I would have felt the joy and complete satisfaction that I feel now.

CHAPTER 16

KEKOA

Twisting around to see the door handle turn, I pluck Shadie off Kai's neck, which she's patiently licking, and roughly shove her resisting, wiggling body into my backpack. Momentary relief floods through me as I see Kalli's ring-clad hand shoot through the opening and hear her explain a procedure to another hospital employee in the hall. She informs the other person she'll just be a second and slips fully through the door, closing it quickly behind her.

"What are you doing in here?" she nervously asks.

"You know I'm in here. I brought you M&M's and you let me in," I respond, thinking all the sugary treats are causing a memory loss.

"No, I mean *what* are you doing? Kai's monitoring machines are changing; his cardio respiratory shot up and now it's slowed below his normal heart rate; his pulse oximeter was showing a consistent downtrend in oxygenation but is now back to normal. Are you messing with the equipment?" she accuses.

"I don't even understand what you're saying, much less have any interest in touching the machines attached to Kai," I retort, but I wonder if Shadie might have been compressing a tube or wire, so I add, "But whatever I might have accidentally done, I'm sorry."

She pauses, and then with a thin smile says, "The thing is, in layman's terms, it's good what happened. It's positive that these changes are registering. It could be a coincidence, or a fluke, but it might have to do with you, a little bit."

Not knowing what to think or do, and not really believing that I could have a positive effect on a kid in a coma, I offer to leave and let her attend to her patient.

As I'm walking to my truck, I think, "I've never really helped anyone, why start now?" Then it registers that I just recently hauled a drowned, unconscious kid to the beach, and I found and brought a slightly mangled dog to a vet. I stayed late yesterday to help one of the other guys on my crew finish hanging cabinets. I gave a tourist an arm to grasp when he was sliding down the trail to Secrets Beach a few days ago when it was a muddy, slippery mess. Hmmmmmm. I don't feel like a sucker or an ass-kisser for going out of my way or offering assistance. If I honestly consider my current state, I notice I actually feel a bit less disheartened about myself and my crappy life than I have in a long time.

CHAPTER 17

KAIMANA

The soft yet solid heating pad under my arm may have had moving parts but how could it also have dog breath? Nothing else smells like dog breath but dog breath. I miss my dog, my buddy, Tickster. He came to me as my fifth birthday present, a poi puppy from the pound, part Lab, part hound; hapa, or mixed plate, like me. I can hear the steady beat of his fat, beaver tail pounding the Ipe planks, welcoming me home. His square head resting on his front paws, saving his energy for the exact moment I throw one of his tennis balls off the raised deck into our yard. Bursting from prone position to long jumper, pre-measured strides to a leaping, "all legs fully extended" super dog flying over the eight steps to the grass and catching the ball on its first bounce. He and I have a bond that rivals any relationship I've had with a human. He senses my energy, as I'm learning to do here, and he can distract me from anything that's bothering me. He adjusts his gait to whatever speed I ride my bike, from slow trot to racing gallop. He adjusts his desires to match mine; beach, surf, watch TV, hoops, skateboard. Whatever I do, he has a role, and he assumes it as if we're the perfect fit on Match.com. His adoration and personality is unconditionally consistent, other than this one time, more than a year ago.

We were cruising with Lono, a friend in Wainiha. His house is up on Powerhouse Road, and we'd race our bikes down the hill way too fast, but somehow we didn't crash, which made it an adventure. Tickster kept up, even if it meant wearing down the pads on his paws, which I would often notice the next day as he gingerly pranced to the beach, staying on the softer grass along the gravel. This day, as we passed one of the local homesteads, a snarling, drooling hundred-pound pit bull barreled toward us. Usually we're able to outride and outrun the pit bulls. They're muscular, aggressive dogs, but not as fast as two kids peddling at a speed to rival the Wicked Witch of the West and paired with a super swift dog like Tickster. On this rainy day, getting outside between downpours, I accidentally ride through a mud-clouded puddle, camouflaging a foot-deep pothole. My front tire lurches down, pulling the handlebars out of my hands, then slams into the front ledge of the gap, launching me over the front of my bike, pounding and rolling my limp body on wet asphalt. The searing pain in my hands and knees, from thumping the street, is shoved aside as I hear the guttural growls and sense in my core the rapidly approaching, deadly dog. Lono is a half-mile past me before he realizes I'm not there, but Tickster executes an Apolo Ohno U-turn and flings his body between the lunging dog and me. Tickster is a peace-loving creature and has never been in a dogfight, yet he charges the pit bull like a trained police dog, barking fiercer than is his nature, sporting a ridge of raised back hair, and puffing up to appear bigger than his gangly forty-five pounds. The pit bull isn't threatened or even slightly deterred. Seeing Tickster only as an object in his path, he pounces, jaws open, on Tick's right shoulder and neck, looking like a great white shark thrashing my dog back and forth. My wild screaming and kicking at the pit bull has no effect, and when I see raw bone exposed on Tickster's side, I realize the other dog is mortally ripping Tick into pieces. I run to the edge of the road looking for a big stick to beat the pit bull with, but I find only lumps of asphalt, which I violently hurl at the battering dog. Years of Little League pay off as one rocky clump hits the pit bull in the side of his flat, ugly face, and with a high-pitched yelp, he releases Tickster, who drops limply to the ground while the bull walks back a few steps. I continue hurling objects at the pit bull, fear and hate fueling my strength. The pit finally scurries back to his yard and I crawl, on bleeding knees, over to Tickster, who lies motionless on the ground.

His right front leg is essentially detached from his shoulder; it lies sideways on his torso at an unnatural angle, hanging on by skin and tendon near his chest. I take off my T-shirt and make a tourniquet around the remaining messy stub. There is blood mixing with the rainwater, turning the puddles around us pink. Nauseated and terrified, I gather up Tickster and stumble toward my friend's house. Hearing my horrified shouts, Lono peddles up the hill, catching the end of the battle, and races ahead to his house. Lono and his dad meet me on the road in their old pickup. Without a word, I jump up on the dropped tailgate; scramble awkwardly to the back of the truck bed, plop down with Tickster in my lap, and yell, "Go, go, take us to the vet." My dog's glazed eyes never leave mine. He is shaking like he's freezing, even though it's eighty-five degrees out. We sit in a puddle of blood and his eyes flutter open and closed. I understand Tick is going to die, but I offer all my strength to him and plead with God to let him hold on. My monologue with my dog steadily continues for the thirty-minute drive to Kapaa's Animal Hospital. As we pull up, I scoop Tick close to my body and jump over the side of the truck bed to jog into the clinic. Thankfully, Lono's dad has called the vet during the drive down and the receptionist expects us; she opens the small gate and leads me back to a surgery room where the vet is waiting.

Dr. Chu has a syringe ready and immediately injects my dog. I feel Tick's shaking begin to slow down and I wonder if he's dead. The doctor asks me to set him on the stainless steel table and unwinds the T-shirt I've wrapped around Tick. The assistant makes a quick gasp when she sees the extent of Tick's gaping wound. There's a fist-size part of his body missing, just gone. His front leg is dangling strangely, just an inch above his leg joint. The vet tells me to wait outside, that he will do all he can to save the dog, but that Tick's chances are slim. I feel the tears burn my eyes, dripping onto my blood-slicked chest as I turn and, with head hanging, slowly walk out of the room.

Three hours later, Dr. Chu emerges and tiredly walks toward me with drooping shoulders. It's obvious this man doesn't talk much, but he hesitantly explains, "His leg was severed through the muscle and bone. It could not be reattached. We amputated what remained and have closed up the wound. He lost a lot of blood, but your dog has the heart of Alemana, the Hawaiian warrior. We will keep him here, and if he makes it through the night, it will offer us hope."

"Can I stay with him? Can I see him?" I plead.

"You can visit him, but he's asleep. Rest is what he needs now," he responds softly, guiding me by the elbow back to the recovery area.

I collapse next to Tick's metal kennel, apologizing profusely for letting this happen, thanking him for saving my life, and telling him, over and over, how much I love him.

He doesn't respond, but after a long stretch of silence, I notice his eyelids faintly fluttering, his muzzle slightly trembling, and his remaining three paws flexing and flicking. I recognize these movements and imagine Tick is dreaming of chasing a chicken. Gradually, sheepishly, his black lips curl up in a half-smirk.

A warm, peaceful sensation floods my body. For the first time since I went over my handlebars four hours ago, I relax.

CHAPTER 18

KEKOA

There are two voice mail messages from Tanita, a woman who claims she is Lulu's owner, which apparently is Shadie's real name. I'm reluctant about returning the dog to her owner, and I resist responding to the call till the evening.

Since I realize I won't have Shadie in my life in the very near future, I take her across the road for one last beach adventure. She sprints the hundred yards across the late afternoon's warm sand and leaps over an ankle-slapper wave into the cerulean water. Pumping her little paws at four different speeds, she spastically swims after the first fish she spies, churning up a small wake behind her. Twenty yards out she's near enough to her prey to attempt a dive. Tucking her snout toward her chest, pulling her front paws in close, she rotates her body forward in a tight ball, and bent tail up, forces her upper torso under the surface. Unlike Shadow, Shadie doesn't breast stroke, she simply dog paddles in a downward direction, diving as much as six feet under water. Delightedly, I observe her every movement as I jog down the beach, launch myself into the silky soft ocean, and swim toward her to get an up-close view of her athletics. We are in four-feet-deep water, skimming along the reefy bottom as she hunts for the angelfish that caught her eye. Underwater, as I'm beside her, she turns her head my way, momentarily off-task, and I swear, she smiles at me. It could be the current moving her lips up, or the force of the water as she swivels her head, but I take this smile as a sign. People see all sorts of signs; the Virgin Mary in tree trunks and UFOs on the roof, but for me, a rescued dog's smile is as meaningful as a burning bush in the desert. In that moment I am hopeful of two things: Kai is going to live, and Shadie is staying with me. There's no Hana Pa'a tonight as Shadie repeatedly dives and misses the angelfish, then tries for a goatfish and needlefish while she bobs over a shallow reef. She walks around on her hind legs, in a foot of water up to her collar, back of her neck stretched taut, chin to chest, giving her a better view of the action swimming below her. There are hundreds of different reef fish at Tunnels; it's her own gigantic aquarium, her version of heaven on earth. As the sun sets, it paints the sky and water in an evolving color splash from pale pinks to violent reds, and Shadie and I shake off and slowly walk back to my messy hut.

I make the dreaded phone call, and I reach Tanita on the first ring.

"Hi, this is Kekoa. I have your dog," I sadly confess.

"Aloooooooha, Kekoooooa, this is Tanita. Mahalo for informing me of Lulu's present location on the earthly plane. I'm currently in the throws of a purification ritual and then will be chanting with my women's group to cast out everything un-wanted and unburden myself with the help of the full moon," she singsongs.

I have no clue what she's talking about, but hearing her desire to "release" something, I ask, "Uh, okay, well, ummmm — is it okay if I keep the dog that you call Lulu? I really like her and she seems to be thriving in the life we have together." I purposely don't mention that I nearly killed her, since I'm guessing that wouldn't warrant much confidence in my pet-ownership skills.

"Oooooooooohhhhh, Kekoooooooooa," she croons blissfully, "the moon has provided the solution. I've been praying that Lulu would find the highest path for herself, in order to be her most fulfilled, enlightened being. This incarnation of the beautiful spirit I call Lulu was not truly meant for me as my incense and candles make her sneeze and she howls when my yoga group 'oms.' Lulu never precisely resonated with my lifestyle."

"Well, I'm happy to keep her. She doesn't seem allergic to my smells, which are mostly a combination of body odor and surf wax, and she enjoys the beach and the ocean, where I spend a lot of time." Without pause and going for the close, I ask, "So can she stay with me forever?"

"Mahalooooooooo, Kekooooooa. You have my blessing. I thank La Luna and am grateful for your strong presence in Lulu's life. Namaste," she crisply concludes, ending our connection.

Snorting laughter bubbles up through my entire body as I crumple to the floor, roll to and swoosh up Shadie in my arms and joyfully inform her, "You're mine!" She responds with one of her not-quite-dog sounds and a dozen sand-papery licks, informing me that she comprehends the situation.

CHAPTER 19

KAIMANA

Back under the water, I feel a fleeting longing for my life on land. There's a freedom down here I've never previously experienced. When did my before-the-coma life become so full of other people's expectations? Expectations of my teachers, coaches, parents, friends, even my three-legged dog, who expects me to take him to the beach every day. Down here, I don't have to be accountable to anyone; I have no responsibilities, chores to do, grades to keep up, heats to win, or future to figure out. There's no one to disappoint, frustrate, or upset. The sea creatures couldn't care less what I do, how I swim, or how I look, and there's a comfort in just hanging out, not doing anything other than being with them.

But I gotta admit, I miss humans. I miss cracking up my friends with one of my dead-on teacher impersonations; making inside jokes with my mom and the way she always forgives me; wrestling around with my dad and his look of pride when I make a big drop or come flying out of a barrel; and teasing that new girl in my science class, the scary-smart one with the green eyes from Maui who just moved here.

I appreciate the underwater world of no expectations, but I miss the closeness and contact above the water. There's a thing that we humans do all the time without even realizing it, sort of like the stranger's connection with the seal. We share something with each other — a mutual feeling of understanding on a level that is a purely human experience. I miss that connection with other people. I have it now more within myself, like I "get" me more than I ever did before. I understand that I pretend to feel, or be, ways I actually don't, just to be accepted. I see that I put most of the pressure I feel on myself just because it's thrilling to win, or to get the best test score. I can acknowledge the part of me that is sometimes lazy, scared, mean, or arrogant and realize we all have parts of us that aren't pretty. I wonder how it would be to accept those parts of myself: Would they take over, or would I be able to be me more fully?

CHAPTER 20

KEKOA

I judged the Irons Brothers Contest the year the kid was in it. That recollection pops into my head as I'm leaving work and passing up a surf session to visit him in the hospital.

He is a little guy, and the youngest one in the nine-to-ten-year-old final. The contest is for all the groms on Kauai and has been a tradition for years. Hundreds of kids sign up, and the first forty-eight entrance forms from each age division are accepted. To make it to the final, a grom has to surf through three six-man heats and place third or better. Six-man heats are difficult because it can turn into a paddling battle more than a surfing battle, but on this contest day there's a two-to-three-foot swell running and Pine Trees has plenty of waves. The kids who have surfed this wave since they were really young have an advantage as it's a bit messy, with odd rips and peaks popping up in less-than-obvious places.

It surprises me how well nine and ten-year-olds surf and this year features a solid crop of amped groms. As the day progresses, I judge dozens of fifteen-minute heats of nine and ten, eleven and twelve-year-old girls, boys, as well as eight and under Menehune (pushed in by parents), and I realize it's challenging to differentiate. There are usually a couple kids in each heat who are clearly better at wave selection, which is as important as ability. There is distinction between groms who can barely catch waves and hesitantly scramble to their feet to make their drop and others who paddle in, pop up, and glide down the wave in one fluid motion. There are a few that can execute soft or slightly jerky turns and often make it through a heat simply by catching waves.

As we approach the end of the day and the finals, I notice one little guy with long, sun-streaked hair who's being coached by his dad. This is a fun contest (not serious stuff like NSSA) and most of the parents are enjoying the sun and the day without getting involved except to take pictures or video. I notice this dad giving a little pep talk to the kid, building his confidence and courage. I feel a tiny burst of envy since I always wanted a dad like that, one who cared about my surfing and came to all my contests instead of playing cards and talking story over a case of beer.

The horn signals the beach start for the last heat of the day, the nine and ten-year-old boys' finals, and the six survivors sprint directly toward the ocean, flinging themselves over the white water, frantically paddling their way out to their pre-chosen spot. The heat is close; there are three boys who are clearly better surfers; two ten-year-olds, and Kai, the scrawny, barely nine-year-old. The two older boys look like shoe-ins for first and second; each has three waves under his belt with scores in the four-to-five range. Kai has one wave, a little insider that he scored a three on by making a couple of nice mid-face turns.

In the judge's tent, which sits on a high plateau on the beach, we see a small set on the horizon and silently hope the boys have enough ocean savvy to paddle out deeper and catch a bigger wave. I watch closely as the pack scrambles for the smaller waves that have been the best choices all day long, but see one grom's head pop up and strain toward the horizon as he senses the approaching set. I continue to score the waves as the boys ride them, and I keep one eye on the red-jersey kid who is paddling out further than anyone has since the first horn at 7:30 a.m. It is now almost 5:00 p.m. and everyone is exhausted, except the adrenalin-pumped kids in the lineup. The other boys in the heat notice the red jersey paddling farther out, and the other five promptly take the shortest path toward the outside breaker that's rumbling its way to land. The judges, all experienced surfers, silently surmise the situation; only one kid has a shot at a set wave, and it is Kai, who still has twenty yards to paddle to make it to the peak before it throws. We all hold our breath for a few seconds, willing his little arms to dig deeper. "Red paddling in," yells the spotter — the person who calls out the colors of the surfer we are to watch and judge — and then "Red up," as Kai turns and strokes into the wave as it crests, gracefully making a drop on the first overhead-to-an-adult wave of the day. "Was that a full roundhouse cutback?" one of the other judges utters unbelievably.

Emerging gracefully from the foam, Kai lays down a bottom turn and shoots straight up the face to the top of the wave, where he confidently hits the lip and throws as much spray as fifty pounds of grom can cast. He executes a few more turns and ends with a small floater, almost surfing onto the sand. A few other groms make it out far enough to catch a shoulder of one of the other set waves, and they also make nice turns and throw their slightly heavier weight around. The horn blows and I turn in my score sheet to the tally girl.

I leave before the trophy presentation, but I know Kai has the victory in the bag with the only 8.5 single-wave score of the day, which gives him the required two-wave-total higher than any other surfer in any other heat.

Now I realize this is the kid, the kid in the coma. I knew I had a vague feeling of seeing him surf before, but I just remembered how watching him surf that day, on that one wave, six years ago, brought me a joy I hadn't felt since I'd left the CT a few years before.

CHAPTER 21

KAIMANA

Mostly I hated English classes. Still, I wish I had a book, even though reading is generally boring. My mind wants to latch onto something other than my inner, liquid world. Even a poetry book would do — though poetry is just annoying because I struggle to understand what the author is trying to say. It seems contrived when words rhyme, but I also get really irritated when they don't. Last quarter, we had to memorize ten lines from one poet. It could have been from ten different poems or from just one. The passages were supposed to share a subject or theme that held personal meaning. The assignment required us to recite the lines in front of the class, which was totally awkward. I chose Rumi, because his was the only poetry book I could find in our house the night before the assignment was due, and I surprised myself by reading dozens of his poems and struggling to narrow down my selection to ten lines from four different poems. Those words now spin in my head.

When the ocean surges,
don't let me just hear it.
Let it splash inside my chest!

Let yourself be silently drawn
by the stronger pull of what you really love.

Don't let your throat tighten with fear.
Take sips of breath all day and night,
before death closes your mouth.

I need more grace
than I thought.

After reciting the lines in class, I confidently declared that Rumi must have been a surfer. Not that there were a lot of waves in Persia, or that surfing was invented yet, but because he captured the way the ocean becomes a part of your body and psyche, how it summons you, how you can't let fear paralyze you, and how it's impossible to imagine how much physical balance and coordination it takes to surf well.

Now, I wonder if Rumi was in a coma. There was another poem I read that I didn't recite, but that I now recall. Something about being " ... in a boat by myself ... I try to stay just above the surface, yet I'm already under and living within the ocean."

WTF? This dude lived my life. Yeah, he was here quite a while ago, like during the thirteenth century, he was a Muslim poet and a Sufi mystic, not exactly a hapa teenager in high school on Kauai. Still, almost a thousand years ago, Rumi understood me.

What if he was clairvoyant and grasped my life better than I do now? What does "I need more grace than I thought" really mean? Maybe it's not physical grace, like body control, but some sort of divine grace, like my mom asks for before she steps in to mediate a thorny arbitration.

What if I need help that isn't the kind of intervention the doctors, or my family, can provide?

CHAPTER 22

KEKOA

On a morning beach jog with Shadie, I get a download (as Shadie's past owner might say) and run home to write it down:

Dear Kauai,

I've been with you my whole life and yet I've never really known you.
Your staggering, stomach-ache-invoking beauty, your luscious, head-swooning smells, your peculiar and silly sounds, your soft, silky smooth air, and your insanely, unbelievably amazing waves.
I often take you for granted, and pass by without acknowledging your magnificence.
Refusing the allure of your seduction.
Keeping myself from allowing your magic to ooze through my senses into my soul.
It scares me, your power and raw charisma.
I fear I'll fall on my knees, drop my forehead to your warm sand, and kiss the ground in rapt appreciation, if I ever really let you in.
The devotion I feel in my heart for you, if I even go there for a second, is so overwhelming, so huge, that I must contain it quickly.
My exquisite Kauai, this is a love letter.

I've never written anything like that before, not sure I've even thought it, any of it.

Somehow, the words just came to me, bubbled up and burst forth like the blowhole on Wainiha Beach.

I notice two voice mail messages from Kalli on my cell phone and hesitate to call her back for fear it's bad news about Kai. He can't leave this place; we're both so absurdly lucky to grow up and live here. There's so much more for him to do, to experience, to feel.

CHAPTER 23

KAIMANA

I miss my sun-drenched, rarely tidy room; my disorganized garage where our surfboards, skateboards, bikes, and fishing poles wait to become the chosen item du jour. I yearn for each piece of gravel that digs into my bare soles as I walk on the side of the road to the beach. I crave my strangely chaotic family; my attached-at-the-heel, hop-along dog; and my often-asinine, volatile friends. Mostly, I deeply ache for the actual ocean, the sensation of untethered, blissed-out buoyancy as I break the surface and the barely noticeable liquid rinses off my day.

I have to feel the moisture-filled, balmy air outside this hospital room on my skin. I need to hear familiar sounds, like geckos laughing, garbage trucks backing up at 3:30 a.m., and hunting dogs excitedly running down the road at midnight. I need to feel river mud squish up between my toes and roll my sweaty skin in warm sand, then wash off every granule with a miniature, eighty-degree wave.

I must get back to the land, and in my body, however messed up it might be.

If I never surf again, I'll deal with it, but I'll desperately need more grace than I thought.

CHAPTER 24

KEKOA

The first message says, "Call me back. It's about Kai."

The second, more urgent message demandingly whines, "Kekoa, call me *now*."

Both messages arrive between 6:00 and 6:15 a.m., which means Kalli must be driving away from her night shift at the hospital. I press "call back" and I'm technologically ushered directly to her voice mail. "Hi, this is Kalli. If you have an emergency, please call 911 or go directly to the ER. If this is personal, please leave me a short message after the beep. Aloha." Her entire message sounds like she blurted it out with just one quick breath. I state my name, tap "end," and set my phone on the bathroom counter, expecting her to call back as I step into the warm water.

Although I'm trying to listen through the deluge, I don't catch the ringtone, and I have a new message from Kalli when I step out to dry off. "Call me back. You're not in trouble, but Kai's doctor wants to talk to you. He knows you've been visiting Kai's room. There's an issue."

I don't press "call back." I feel nauseated, like when I used to get summoned to the principal's office in high school and had no idea what I was going to get in trouble for, but I was usually ready to take the fall for one of my friends since my dad never showed up when he got called and I signed off on any notes that were sent home to him. I realize I wasn't supposed to be in the Intensive Care area, but why would the doctor want to talk to me? Wouldn't they just give me an ICU trespassing ticket, or make me do community service, like hang out with the really old sick guys who think World War II is still happening?

Stepping into my work jeans, I remind myself I'm a grown-up and that I'm able to speak with a doctor, even if it means taking a verbal wrist slapping. I don't need Kalli's pep talk, I'll just take the doctor's call when it happens and deal with it.

Driving toward my jobsite, Shadie contently curled up in the passenger seat, my techno ringtone pounds out a beat to let me know I'm receiving a call from "unknown." It's a Lihue prefix, so it must be the doc.

"Hi, this is Kekoa," I defensively answer.

Briskly, the caller says, "Kekoa, this is Stephen Tanaka, Kaimana Keller's doctor. Do you have a few minutes to talk?"

Hesitantly, I reply, "Sure, I guess."

He proceeds, "We are aware that you have been spending time in Kaimana's room. Other than the fact that this is against hospital rules, there is other provocative information that has arisen in our recent review of Kai's condition during the time frames that you were visiting."

"Um, OK," I stammer.

"Are you available to come by my office today, around noon, to discuss?" he asks.

"Well, not really. I work all day on the North Shore and I only take an hour for lunch, which means I couldn't get to Lihue and back with any time to talk to you," I reply, hoping to get out of a meeting with the work-obligation argument.

His tone evolves from brisk to brusque as he asks, "Do you realize there is a boy's life at stake? Kai has been in a coma for more than a month. We've used the latest clinical tools for measuring the depth of a coma, but Kai has consistently been nonresponsive in two of the four categories, eye and motor. He has been able to breathe on his own, but over the past week, he has shown increased signs of needing a breathing tube. His brain stem reflexes have shown the lowest possible rating to allow basic body functioning. Yet, when we reviewed his complete printouts, there are three times that his brain stem reflexes have shown increased activity, which correlate with your visits, and once his PET scan showed increased brain metabolism, which also correlate with tests completed shortly after you were in the room with the patient. In our staff meeting this morning, we called in the doctors and nurses to discuss Kai's situation and the possibility that he is moving toward a permanent vegetative state. We may need to begin considering end-of-life discussions with his parents. We've compiled all the data and given a brief report to each doctor. At this point, I noticed the variances and asked if anyone had any idea what was going on during those few times we saw slightly increased brain activity. Kalli admitted that she allowed you access to Kai's room. We've informed Kai's parents and they're not pressing charges. In fact, they've asked me to speak with you. Kalli is in trouble for not maintaining hospital code, but as head of the department and Kai's doctor, I'm willing to forgive her transgressions if you will work with me to help us determine if there is any chance for Kai's recovery before we begin moving in the other direction."

As I hang an illegal U-turn and rapidly head toward the hospital, breaking another law, I ask, "Are you available to meet in thirty minutes?"

CHAPTER 25

KAIMANA

I sense a great deal of chaotic energy in my room. The noise is a human buzz of voices, and it sounds like multiple conversations about a just-seen movie. I don't listen, as nothing that anyone has done or said has helped me in any way.

Just as I'm spiraling down into my own depths, one tone catches my attention. I've never heard his voice in combination with anyone else's. I sometimes wonder if I create him; the stranger-surfer. I hook into his lilt, the laid-back, slightly pidgin way he speaks, and hone in on his energy like a laser. I wonder if he possesses a lifeline that only he can toss. I'm not sure if it's for him or me. I sense he's saving himself, burning down the imagined hau bush that surrounds and keeps him from others, blowing away the low-pressure weather that forces his emotions and feelings to stay limited and controlled, pushing through his internal barriers that keep him from seeing his own life as magical and remarkable. Somehow I recognize I've contributed to his changes, in some small, inexplicable way.

He nears me and assumes his regular bedside position, but doesn't speak, just like the first time he came to my room.

I wait.

Those "Try Wait" bumper stickers used to really piss me off. I mean, I had places to go, surf to check, friends to meet, and it never failed that the car in front of us, going fifteen mph through Hanalei, was yet another wannabe local with "Live Aloha," "Eddie Would Go," "Ainokea," "Pray for Surf," and "Try Wait" stickers plastered all over the rusted bumper of a dirty Toyota Celica.

In my unwelcome "try wait" state, I hang out and concentrate on the stranger in hopes that the lifeline isn't exclusively for him.

CHAPTER 26

KEKOA

Comprehending most of what the doctor has explained to me, I tentatively attempt to talk to Kai. Fewer than one sentence makes it out of my mouth before I turn and utter, "You all have to leave. I can't talk in the way I have before with everyone in here. I don't know what I said, or what I'm going to say, but it definitely doesn't feel the same with people around."

Dr. Tanaka announces, "Everyone, please step outside. Let's leave Kekoa and Kai alone for a while." Then he quietly says to me, "We'll be watching Kai's monitors. I'll tap lightly on the door if there are any changes."

I feel extremely self-conscious. What am I supposed to say or do? I want Kai to get better, but just because my voice, or the stories I've told him in the past, has caused his brain to perk up a little doesn't mean I can pull him out of the coma. I'm not even sure why I'm here, why I'm making the effort.

A memory I had forgotten, although it was just two short months ago, inundates my consciousness, so for lack of other material, I uncomfortably share it with Kai.

"I am surfing Pila'a at sunset. The two other surfers, who braved the huge swell, monstrous current, and low tide, have just hiked up the dirt trail, leaving me alone in the water, searching for a blue-black bump to catch and transport me nearer to shore. As the sky quickly dims, and waves become less and less discernable, I know I am out of time and need to catch something soon or risk, among other things, becoming shark bait. Pila'a is generally a lumbering, mean wave when it's working, and today it's on the job and angry. As a dark mound rises behind me, I hurriedly paddle into a bomb and struggle to blindly find my way down the face of the wave as I make the murky drop. Too steep to grab rail, I drop top-to-bottom, and as I slightly hold back on my usual broad bottom-turn, I feel my inside fin hit something hard, a rock or a turtle. My board jerks left, my rail digs into the wave and I'm whiplashed off my board, face first into the shadowy sea. Falling so early on a wave can mean trouble, and this is no exception as the full force of the frothing lip pile-drives me to the rocky bottom, where I manage to curl up in a tight ball and attempt to 'roll with it.' It's a menacing, prolonged hold-down and I know I need a gulp of air to handle the next wave, but as the pressure releases and I start to swim toward the surface, I punch my extended hands directly into the ocean floor. Realizing I am back-asswards, I quickly somersault, push off a large boulder, and shoot toward the only other possible surface. Just as my fingers break through to air, and my hope for a gasp of oxygen becomes intense, the sickening slam of another wave's lip impacts directly on top of me. I'm pushed deep into the blackness with no air and I fight the increasing terror of losing consciousness.

"Strangely, rather than my panic fueling me with the strength to attempt to fight my way through the downward force, the fear washes through me, and I'm overcome with complete calm.

"I realize absolutely that I will die this night, on the bottom of the ocean, unbeknownst to anyone.

"Instead of regret, remorse or anger, I'm flooded with a feeling of what I can only describe as absolute love. I feel totally connected to the ocean, to all the sea creatures, to everything; I'm at peace with my choice to continue to be a surfer, to surf in dangerous conditions alone at sunset. I somehow take a moment to acknowledge that when I surf I am as happy as I have ever been in my life. I open my arms wide, unfurled from protecting my body, and I embrace my life, my choices, and my imminent death.

"I don't know what happens next, because those are the last actions and thoughts I remember.

"Somehow, I find myself on the shore without a scratch or cut on me and without a single new ding on my board. I have no idea how I got there. I sit for a while, maybe an hour, under the starless night sky, not really aware of my body, but clearly alive and on the beach. Eventually, shivering from the cold, I slowly climb up the trail to my truck, drive home, shower, and go to bed."

I glance at Kai. Nothing. No movement. No tapping on the door. No change. I stand up to leave, but pause when I realize I haven't thought of that night until now. It was too scary and inexplicable to even tolerate in my conscious thoughts. I do remember wondering why I was allowed to live. Why me? I didn't want to admit that the only explanation, and it's even totally questionable, is that something saved me. Something or someone (like what, an angel?) lifted me off the bottom of the ocean and dragged my body and board through the shore-pound, rocks and reef, and up twenty rugged yards onto the beach. It makes no sense and I feel unworthy of this benevolent gesture from the universe.

For the past few years, I've believed that my life was basically over. That any contribution I was going to make had passed me by. I've never loved anyone. I've never even deeply cared about anyone, even myself. The only thought that occurs to me is that maybe I was meant to live so I could help save Kai, this boy with his whole life in front of him. Maybe he wasn't meant to die satisfied, in the water, taken out by a coconut in a barrel. Maybe he isn't meant to fade slowly away and let his life ooze out of him as he gives up and takes whatever is handed to him.

CHAPTER 27

KAIMANA

I can barely make out what the surfer is saying. I pick up on some short phrases, but I'm so far under, so deep in the thick fluid of my own ocean that I can't understand his story.

I sense he is making deep changes in his beliefs and his outlook on life. It's like he's rewiring his mind, figuring out how to cut a new trail. Like surfing switch-foot, your body and brain feel all discombobulated, totally awkward. As if you've never been upright and flowing on a surfboard in your life. Yet, if you go switch-foot over and over, somehow moving through the embarrassment and kookiness of it, you start to feel OK doing something totally differently from what you originally learned and were completely comfortable doing. Eventually, you can even make a turn or pull into a barrel with the wrong foot forward.

I don't understand where I'm going or how to change or transform anything that's happening to me. I desperately want to live, to regain consciousness, to move forward with my life, but there is no effort that I haven't tried to use to accomplish that. From his story, the only idea that floats through my thoughts is, "The ocean giveth, and the ocean taketh away."

CHAPTER 28

KEKOA

A tap on the door pulls me from my reverie. I stand still, waiting for another signal. I'm spent, exhausted, and I don't know what else to say or do. After a half hour of silence, the doctor opens the door, poking his head through, and asks me to step outside the room.

"There was a slight improvement in Kai's condition when you were speaking. In layman's terms, he was paying attention to you. This is a good sign," the doc offers.

I notice the inflection at the end of his comment and say, "But … "

"But, overall, his condition is worsening. He's showing less and less brain activity. His own drive to breathe is weak and he will soon need the breathing tube. His kidneys are deteriorating." The doctor finishes the assessment telling me what I suspected, but do not want to hear.

"I guess I should leave then. It doesn't seem I can help. I'm sorry," I mutter, as I turn to go in dejection.

As I pass through the ICU doorway, a woman absentmindedly bumps my arm as she enters. I recognize Kai's mom from the photos on the blog. She seems to know who I am, maybe from my time on the tour, and weakly smiles and says, "Hi, Kekoa."

We stop, stalled in the doorway, and look at each other. I can feel her sadness, the weight pressing down on her small frame as she approaches her nonresponsive son. She's not that much older than me, but she's wearing every year of her life in the creases of her concerned forehead. Her eyes telegraph her undying love for Kai and her unwillingness to let him go. I never had this force in my life. I can't imagine what it might feel like to have another human dedicated to my safety, well-being, and happiness. To care so deeply, to love and support without boundaries, to never give up on me.

And, then, I get it. I understand why I'm the one person that might be able to help Kai. He doesn't know how to make it in the world on his own. He doesn't need to know. He has loving parents. He's a kid. He'll figure it out eventually, when he's off at college or on his own, surfing remote Indo. But I know how to scrap and fight my way out of trouble. I knew how to make meals for myself when I was five. I taught myself how to surf. I went door-to-door and asked to do yard work so I could make enough money to take a girl on a date. I ironed my own high school graduation gown and congratulated myself on my simple scholastic accomplishment. I have figured out every single thing in life on my own. Not that I've done it right, or even well, but I have the internal fortitude and survival techniques that it takes to stay alive, alone, on my own, without help. And even though I have this insight, I don't know what to do with it.

I feel helpless, but I have a small clue, as I gently brush past Mrs. Keller and head to the source of all insight, the ocean.

CHAPTER 29

KAIMANA

When did I stop appreciating my life? The continual encouragement and care from my parents; the spectacular sights of my island home; the goofy goodness of my friends; the sweet adoration of my little sister; the slobbering reverence of my dog; the astonishingly "if not always perfect, always fun" waves; even my not-very-academic but often-entertaining high school? What turned off that gratitude sensor in me? To see, hear, taste, touch, and feel all the beauty, love, fun, and adventure that my little life is made up of? I'm fifteen years old, and I'm a cynical old man. I make fun of people surfing. I swear at tourists crossing the street too leisurely or driving painfully slow to stare at a waterfall. I am frequently unkind and intolerant of my sister and my dog, simply because they interrupt me while watching TV. I complain about my dad's loud, cryptic orders to help around the house and yard. I meanly tease my mom about her hair, her clothes, her surfing, her singing, and just about anything she says around my friends. I've chosen to be critical and to judge others harshly as my standard practice.

And here I am ...

Caught inside myself with all my regrets and the awareness that none of those skeptical comments ever did anything but hurt or upset the people they were directed at. I suppose I felt, momentarily, better or cooler. Maybe one of my friends would laugh, maybe the humiliated beginner surfer would flail to the beach, leaving the break I was surfing, maybe my sister or dog would skulk out of the room, maybe I'd get released from taking out the garbage cans, maybe my mom would stop humming. Other than the ceasing of my mom's horrible singing, all the other results didn't really benefit me and were at someone else's expense. It doesn't make me feel good about myself, that's for sure, or that my presence is a positive, or would be missed as a constructive force on earth.

CHAPTER 30

KEKOA

After a rejuvenating surf and a quick swim with
Shadie, we both shake off and jump in the truck
for the long drive to the hospital.

Taking advantage of my permission to enter, I
breeze through the ICU guard station, say "hi"
to the non-Kalli nurse, and slide into Kai's
room. It's late, maybe 11:00 p.m., so I'm alone
with Kai.

Not really sure how to address him, I begin,
"Dude, grom, Kai, brah, hey! You gotta listen
to me."

Without acknowledgment, I continue, "I don't
know how to say this nicely, but you gotta
pull your head out of your ass. Seriously. You
have the cherry life. You have everything I
never had, as well as everything I did have.
Maybe you already know this and you're beating
yourself up about being a little shit, which you
probably were a good deal of the time. You're a
teenager. You live in Hanalei. You surf. You're
a good-looking kid. You're smart and do well in
school. You've got a solid family. You probably
have more than three surfboards. You go on nice
vacations. And, let me guess, you take it all
for granted? Well, so does everyone who has
it all. But, some, a few, wake up and realize

if they're not making a positive contribution every day, they're making a negative one.

"You can choose to use the luck of the draw that's given you this particularly cushy life and still do something of value in the world. Maybe you'll surf the tour and be another world champion from Kauai, without those issues that killed the other one. Maybe you'll be a surgeon and fix athletes who get injured so they can continue playing the sport they love. Maybe you'll be an artist and bring your clients joy through your painting, or help them achieve business success through your graphic designs. Maybe you'll fall in love, get married and be an even better husband and father than the really good dad you have. There is something else, though, that you gotta know.

"You have something more than just all the right people, stuff, and opportunity. You can surf. And not just a little. You have an amazing gift. Guys surf their whole life — great athletes take up surfing and dedicate themselves to it — and they will never, ever make a bottom turn with that much speed, or hit the lip as vertically, or float smoothly over thirty feet of foam, or land an air reverse effortlessly, or make a huge drop and rail slide into a perfect barrel, like you do on a daily basis. There are thirty million surfers in the world and you're already in the top one percent. Tourists will have photos of you on their Facebook vacation pages back in Kansas, girls will want to meet you and will cut you a lot of slack to be who you are, your friends and grown men will be jealous of your style, your talent, your ability, and your execution.

"You are a surfer. A really, really exceptional surfer. It's magical. It's rare. It's a gift. And since you have this endowment from the universe bestowed on you, you owe it to yourself to come back and share it with the rest of us. Because even though I might be envious of your ability, I will always feel a touch of awe and joy when I get the opportunity to watch you surf, to be in the water with you, to share the experience at the level that only great surfers understand, because I have it too, and I never actually accepted that fact until now.

"The strange thing is: it's not even really about the act of surfing. It's about the essence of surfing: the flow, the oneness with the wave and the universe, the absolute freedom, the sense of extreme gratitude, and the continual humbling that surfing provides. Surfing teaches you how to be in the world, if you just listen."

Startling myself with my speech, I feel a little like an Academy Awards winner who's gone over his two-minute allowance and I quickly usher myself off the stage of his room and walk briskly back to the humid, dog-breath-infused cab of my truck.

CHAPTER 31

KAIMANA

I heard every word.

I have not been focused for that long since I arrived here. I held my breath, waiting for him to pause, so I could slide back under water, but he never stopped until he left.

As I fully absorb his words, I feel something like pride. Not arrogance. Maybe dignity. It's a humble, thankful sensation. More than anything, I feel worthy. Gratefulness permeates my cells. I feel a burning flame in my core that's giving me strength and power. Not the usual kind, either. This is something truer, more eternal and real.

And it strikes me that sometimes, even though I hate it, I know I have to go back in, to get through it.

Like digging wana out of my foot, it hurts to poke around in the tender pad, but until I remove that little speck of sea urchin, my foot won't heal. It's also like the time the tide and swell rose alarmingly fast while I was exploring a sea cave on the Na Pali Coast and had to heave myself through the raging, water-swollen, rocky mouth to get back to daylight. It reminds me of when I swam up from a wipeout with the sickening awareness that my leash was hooked on a coral head and I had to force my oxygen-deprived head back underwater to unhook the Velcro and free myself. These experiences encourage me to go back in, to move through it.

I'm paddling out at a nearly empty Pine Trees, the nose of my board cutting through dirty water, and I hear the whistle and know a big set is coming. I hustle for the peak that the others let pass, I stroke hard and drop in as I feel the rapture and thrill of that last perfect barrel. I force myself to stay alert and I absorb the impact of the heavy coconut as it hits my head. I fully sense the pain and shock that presses the much-needed air from my lungs, which thoroughly overwhelms me underwater and causes me to surrender in defeat and reject my consciousness. But instead, this time, I let the terror wash over and through me; I feel it, hold it, know absolutely that I'm in trouble and will probably die, but I stay present anyway and it's just me and my fear, hanging out. Eventually, slowly, the fear runs it course and recedes. I plant my feet on the hard sand of the ocean floor, lunge deeply, and rocket myself to the surface, burst through to foamy air, gulp a desperately needed nip of oxygen, open my eyes wide, and yell, "Help me!"

EPILOGUE

On February 28th, six weeks after Kaimana Keller was rushed unresponsive to ICU by ambulance, he opened his eyes, shouted two words, and began his slow recovery from his injury and coma.

Over the next two months of rehabilitation, with the support of speech and physical therapists, Kai slowly regained language and motor skill functioning. Eventually, he was seen jogging the soft, deep sand at Lumahai, swimming into Hanakapiai, and hiking back to Ke'e Beach, free-diving the outer reef at Tunnels, and silently practicing yoga on the beach at dawn, often in the company of an older, dark-skinned companion and two dogs. The vibrantly fit athletes were sometimes overheard discussing the ridiculously amazing beauty of Kauai and the thrilling adventures they shared.

During the spring season on the North Shore of Kauai, as only locals anticipate, an unpredicted, three-foot, glassy NW swell arrived in the last week of April. Almost four months after Kai's accident, he picked up his board, slid it under his arm, and slowly walked the five short blocks to the beach.

On a surfboard for the first time since January, Kai paddled out at Pine Trees, paused twenty yards to the side of the break, sat up on his board, and watched the early-morning surfers catch waves. After half an hour, his new friend paddled out and serenely sat next to him, talking story for another hour. When his parents asked him later what made him wait all that time, Kai mumbled, "I was totally afraid to paddle for a wave, because, what if?"

Kai sat in the channel, trembling from chill and self-doubt, but with a newfound acceptance of life without surfing. A rogue wave swung wide past the surfers in the lineup, and to those watching on the beach, appeared to offer Kai a "now or never" opportunity.

After a three-stroke paddle-in and a slightly wobbly drop, Kai micro-adjusted his feet on the deck of his favorite shortboard. With accelerating speed, he proceeded to lay down a gorgeous, sweeping bottom turn, shoot perpendicularly vertical, hit the lip with complete abandon, and throw six feet of spray over the top of the wave and onto the smiling surfer paddling by, Kekoa Jones.

GLOSSARY OF HAWAIIAN SURFING WORDS AND PLACES (IN ORDER AS THEY APPEAR)

Hawaiian method for determining wave height: Wave size is measured from the back of the wave. It usually results in an estimation less than half that of a face measurement. A wave described as "four foot" has a wave face of at least eight to ten feet. Coming into use during the 1960s, the Hawaiian method apparently was adopted as psychological intimidation of inexperienced visitors.

Surfline: When started, Surfline was a continuously updated phone recording and is now a real-time website that provides "know before you go" information on surf forecasts, including the size and quality of swells approaching and hitting many surf spots around the world.

Menehune: Hawaiian mythological dwarfs who live in the forests or hidden valleys.

Pine Trees: Beach break in Hanalei Bay. Between The Cape and Retro's. Depending on the shape of the sand bar and swell direction, the break varies from gently playful to expert-level surfing.

Grom: Shortened from grommet, a young surfer (usually under sixteen) who is not necessarily a beginner and often rips.

Musubi: Popular snack food in Hawaii comprised of rice, spam, and soy sauce wrapped in seaweed paper.

Manalau: Outside reef break, behind Pine Trees, in Hanalei Bay. Swell must be producing waves of at least four feet (Hawaiian) for Manalau to bump, feather, or break. Also called Monster Mush.

Kook: One of the most hurtful words to be called by a surfer. It means you can't surf well, have a terrible style, and make uncool mistakes while in the water attempting to surf.

Andy (Irons): Three-time world champion professional surfer on the World Championship Tour. The only surfer to have won a title at every venue on the ASP calendar. Andy died of cardiac arrest, reportedly caused by an accidental drug overdose. The surfing world, Kauai surfers, and groms particularly were devastated by the news of his death. In honor of Andy's life, over ten thousand surfers, fans, family, and friends attended a Hanalei Bay paddle-out.

The Tour or CT (World Championship Tour): Now called the ASP World Tour, in which the thirty-four top-ranked surfers in the world compete at twelve contests worldwide for the opportunity to become world champion.

Bruce (Irons): Andy Irons's younger brother who often beat Andy in contests as they were growing up and into their early twenties (but Andy proved a tougher competitor once they were both on the ASP world tour). Winner of the Pipe Masters and the Eddie Aikau, Bruce no longer surfs on the ASP or CT, but accepts wild-card opportunities for special events. He is regarded as one of the best free surfers and barrel riders in the world.

Junior Pro: The training/feeding grounds for the QS and CT, a series of contests for competitors who are twenty years and under.

QS (World Qualifying Series): Scheduled surf contests with rankings of one to six stars that allow surfers to accumulate points to qualify for the WCT/ASP World Tour. Now called Star and Prime events.

NSSA (National Scholastic Surfing Association): A nonprofit organization whose mission is to encourage and assist its members in their interest to learn and develop the fundamentals and skills of surfing competition while competing in structured and quality events. It is the only statewide contest format for young Hawaiian surfers. Surfers, beginning at age ten and under, compete against other surfers on Oahu, Maui, Big Island, and Kauai each year in a series of contests taking place throughout the state. Each season culminates in Regional Championships, where a surfer's scores added to his or her top five contest results determine who is invited to participate in the NSSA National Championships in Southern California.

Lowers: Surfbreak within Trestles, which is a collection of surf spots at San Onofre State Beach, just south of San Clemente.

Salt Creek: Three Surfbreaks just south of the city of Laguna Niguel in Orange County.

The Cape: Surfbreak between Pine Trees and the Pavilion in Hanalei Bay, Kauai.

Mark Foo: Professional big wave surfer from Oahu, Hawaii. Mark drowned while surfing Maverick's.

Mavericks: Surf break a half mile off Half Moon Bay on the northern California coast. Called the Mount Everest of surfing.

Nightmarchers: Ghosts of ancient Hawaiian warriors who are believed to march at sunset and just before the sun rises. Legend warns if a person looks in the nightmarcher's eyes as they pass, the nightmarchers will take the person with them.

Kahuna: A wise and trained professional, often a priest or healer with deep knowledge of Hawaiian culture, lore, and spiritual practices.

Ho'oponopono: An ancient Hawaiian practice of reconciliation and forgiveness. The process of Ho'oponopono is to align with and clean up ones genealogy and relationships with other people. Essentially, it means to make it right with the ancestors, or to make right with the people with whom you have relationships. It is believed that the original purpose of Ho'oponopono was to correct the wrongs that had occurred in someone's life, including Hala (to miss the thing aimed for, or to err, to disobey) and Hewa (to go overboard or to do something to excess), which were illusions, and even 'Ino (to do harm, implying to do harm to someone with hate in mind), even if accidental. Sometimes called the Hawaiian Code of Forgiveness.

Pono: There are eighty-three English translations of Pono. The most common are goodness, morality, correct or proper procedure, righteous, right, and virtuous. In Hawaii, and among Hawaiians, the word has strong cultural and spiritual connotations of "a state of harmony or balance."

Puka's: A fast, hollow, dangerous reef beach break at Haena Beach Park. The word literally translates as "hole." The beach break is called Puka's because the wave is hollow, like a hole.

Bethany (Hamilton): Young surfer who lost her left arm to a shark attack at Tunnels. She recovered from injury and surfs professionally, as well as wrote Soul Surfer, a book also made into a movie, and is an inspiration to all who know her.

Black Pot: Beach park and local gathering spot behind the Hanalei Pier and parking lot. Called Black Pot after a big black wok owned by Henry Tai Hook, who used to cook community meals here in the late 1800s.

OxyContin: Highly addictive, widely abused painkiller synthesized from opium-derived Thebaine. Also called Ocycodone or Oxy.

Akikiki: Small, energetic honeycreeper (bird) endemic to the island of Kauai; presently on the verge of extinction.

(Kelly) **Slater:** Eleven-time ASP World Champion surfer, including five consecutive titles. Both the youngest (twenty) and oldest (thirty-nine) to win the world title. To date, he has forty-eight world championship tour victories. Often said to have a magical relationship with the ocean, conjuring a set wave to ride, often to "steal" the win from his competitor, with seconds left in the heat.

Hanalei: Spectacularly beautiful valley and quaint beach town sitting on Hanalei Bay, surrounded by taro fields and the Namolokama Mountain Range. Located on the north shore of Kauai.

Pidgin: Simplified or "broken" form of English language used in Hawaii, primarily by locals.

Anini: Beach park between Kilauea and Princeville, Kauai. One of two legal campgrounds on the north shore of Kauai.

Haena Beach Park: One of the most northern beach parks on Kauai, located on Makua Bay, commonly called Tunnels.

Bordered by two large reef systems creating expert-only winter surf and premier summer snorkeling.

Koa: Hawaiian hardwood, used originally for outrigger canoes and surfboards. Used in high-end custom homes for cabinetry, floors, and trim.

Kauapea Road: Ocean bluff road in Kilauea, Kauai with less than twenty home sites, each with 180 degree+ unblocked ocean views. Above Secret Beach (most homes have their own private trail down the one thousand foot cliff to the sand below).

Secret Beach: Surrounded by high cliff walls with long stretches of sand punctuated by exposed lava reef and view of Kilauea, Kauai lighthouse. Ruggedly stunning with beach and reef surf breaks along Kauapea Bay. A fifteen-minute steep and often slippery hike from dirt parking lot.

Sunset Beach: Famous, open-ocean reef surf break on the north shore of Oahu. Known for big winter waves, strong current, and challenging surf.

The Bay: Term used for the three breaks (The Point, Flatrock, and The Bowl) that are reef-bottom, right point breaks off the northern tip of Hanalei Bay, Kauai.

Majors (Bay): Surfbreak on the west side of Kauai. Accessible via Pacific Missile Range Facility a naval military base five miles from Kekaha.

Tunnels: Expert-only, outer reef surf break consisting of three distinct breaks: Dump Trucks, The Killing Floor, and West Reef. Tunnels acquired its name from the surfers who have seen the tube and divers who have found the caverns. Located in Makua Bay, Haena, Kauai.

Pancho (Sullivan): Born in Haena, Kauai but known for his power surfing on the north shore of Oahu. Said to "displace more water than twenty men" when throwing spray on a turn.

Flatrock: One of three reef breaks at The Bay. Between The Point and The Bowl, it is known for steep drops and fast barreling sections.

Haole: Caucasian person, or any foreigner or non-Hawaiian local. Literally meaning "no breath," implying foreigners have no spirit or life within. Often used derogatorily.

Ahi: Hawaiian term for yellow-fin tuna weighing over one hundred pounds.

Poi dog: Poi is a Hawaiian staple food made from taro. Poi dog refers to a breed of dog that lived on vegetables, like poi, but has evolved to a slang meaning a mixed breed of dog common in Hawaii, often having hound or hunting dog qualities.

Makaha: Right point surf break over reef and sand on the west side of Oahu. Famous for good waves and gnarly locals.

Rell Sunn: Pioneer in women's surfing and the first female lifeguard in Hawaii. Diagnosed with breast cancer and given one year to live, she continued to surf daily and became an advocate and educator for women's awareness about cancer. She lived another fourteen years. Remembered as the "Queen of Makaha."

Brian Keaulana: Born and raised at Makaha, the son of Buffalo Keaulana. A famous Hawaiian surfer and lifeguard.

Kewalo's: Surf break in Kewalo's Basin, on the south side of Oahu, where NSSA Regional Championships are usually held.

Alamoana Bowls: Fast, left surf break in Waikiki, Oahu, across the channel from Alamoana Beach Park, where HASA State Championships are usually held.

Backside: For a regular-foot surfer, going left on a wave. For a goofy-foot surfer, going right on a wave.

Middles: Open ocean, primarily left reef break in the middle of Hanalei Bay, Kauai.

Queens: Outer reef break, beyond Hanalei Bay's perimeter. In order for Queen's to break, the swell must be above high surf advisory and producing waves with faces over twenty feet.

Nene: Also called the "Hawaiian Goose," it is endemic to Hawaii and the official state bird. Currently one of the rarest creatures on earth.

Gerry Lopez: In the seventies and eighties, he was widely recognized as the best tuberider in the world and won the Pipeline Maters in 1972 and 1973. He wrote an anecdotal, autobiographical book titled *Surf Is Where You Find It.* Known as Mr. Pipeline.

(Banzai) **Pipeline:** Famous expert left surf break off Ehukai Beach Park in Pupukea on the north shore of Oahu. There are three reefs at Pipeline in progressively deeper water further out to sea that activate according to the increasing size of approaching ocean swells.

Retro's: Beach break between Pine Tree's and Grandpa's in Hanalei Bay, Kauai.

Hokule`a: Polynesian double-hulled voyaging canoe. Best known for her 1976 Hawaii-to-Tahiti voyage performed with only Polynesian navigation techniques and without any modern navigational instruments (no watches, compasses, sexton, GPS, or instrumentation).

Hihimanu: Hihimanu is the Hawaiian word for Mana Ray, and the mountain is aptly named because with its twin peaks it resembles a Mana Ray tail. Part of a long ridge leading to Namolokama, which at 4,423 feet is one of the largest freestanding mountains in Hawaii. Hihimanu divides the valley behind Hanalei from the Upper Hanalei River Valley.

Hapa: A person of mixed Asian or Pacific Islander racial ethnic heritage. Also used loosely to describe anyone of mixed ethnicity or part white. Literally translates as "portion" or "part."

Wainiha: Small community, primarily local, located between Hanalei and Haena, Kauai.

Hana Pa'a: Hawaiian word that literally translates as "to fasten or secure" but is used by fishermen to announce a fish is on the hook.

Namaste: East Indian salutation. Derived from Sanskrit, it means, "I salute or recognize your presence or existence in society and the universe."

Hau Bush: Indigenous plant in Kauai. It grows from seven to thirty feet tall. It has heart-shaped leaves, and flowers that last for one day. The branches grow close to the ground and all intertwine and tangle with each other, making it prolific and difficult to remove.

Na Pali (Coast): Sixteen rugged miles of coast on Kauai's northwest shore with sea cliffs soaring up to four thousand feet vertically from the ocean. Sometimes mentioned as the eighth Great Wonder of the world.

Lumahai: Picturesque beach between Hanalei and Haena, Kauai, where scenes of the movie *South Pacific* were filmed.

Pila'a: Remote, rocky, expert-only surf break between Kilauea and Moloa'a, on the southeastern edge of the north shore.

Wana: The Hawaiian name for the sea urchin (pronounced as vana).

Hanakapiai: Hanakapiai Beach is approximately two miles from the start of the Kalalau Trail. During summer months, Hanakapiai Beach's sandy shoreline is clearly visible; during winter months, dangerously powerful waves and high tides wash away the sandy shoreline. The beach is remotely located with no road access.

Ke'e: Beach at the end of the road in Haena. Located at the farthest point one can drive going northwest on Kauai. Marks the start of the Kalalau Trail.

READER S GUIDE

1. How are Kaimana's and Kekoa's attitudes and personalities similar? Different?

2. How do the dogs (Shadow, Shadie/Lulu, Tickster) affect Kai and Kekoa?

3. Describe similarities and differences between Kai's and Kekoa's fathers?

4. How do you imagine Kekoa's life would have differed had he not saved Kai?

5. If Kekoa had not visited and talked to Kai, do you think Kai would have come out of the coma? Why or why not?

6. Which surfing story of Kekoa's resonated with you the most? Why?

7. In the surfing story you chose (above), what was the lesson? How does that lesson apply to your own life?

8. Are you more similar to Kai or Kekoa? Explain by comparing examples from your own life with some in the book.

9. How might Kai have changed since his accident and recovery? How might his life be different due to these changes? How has your life changed due to a traumatic experience?

10. How might Kekoa have changed since his involvement in Kai's accident and recovery? How might his life be different due to these changes? How has your life changed due to your involvement in someone else's traumatic experience?